OUT OF THE DEPTHS

David James

Dedicated to the memory of
Jennefer Tobin MBE
19th April 1944 – 18th August 2023

Tireless worker for the safety of Merchant Navy seafarers,
founder of a charity for
the rehabilitation of injured service people
and
owner of 17 Wilkes Street for many years.

A good friend and shipmate.

Also by David James

A Flower in Winter
Book 1 of the
Flower in Winter Trilogy

Reviews for *A Flower in Winter:*

… a polished piece of careful and diligent research, detailed scene-setting, suspense building through atmospheric descriptions while always involving believable characters knit together by very fine writing. I hope for more of the same from [this author] as he clearly has the novelist's touch: what a pity that we have had to wait for so long [for his debut]…

Lt-Col Ewan Southby-Tailyour OBE RM (Retd)
Royal Cruising Club's Spring magazine, Tidings 2025

This book is superbly written. An incredible amount of research has obviously been undertaken. It's unusual for such a book to be an easy read - but it is! When I'd finished, I felt like I had been absorbed into a first-class film. Highly recommended!

Caroline Schofield
Amazon

A letter to my publisher

25 July 2025

Ian Hooper
Director
Leschenault Press
Western Australia

Dear Ian

Shortly after the publication of *A Flower in Winter,* a parcel arrived containing a badly typed manuscript. An anonymous note was attached:

Dear Mr Gale, as no-one mentioned in this story is still alive, perhaps it could now be published?

I have retyped the manuscript in the hope that you agree and called the story after my belief that the souls of sailors rise again in gulls.

Psalm 130 provides another reason for the title: *Out of the depths have I cried unto thee, O Lord.*

Philip Gale

Prologue

My mother, Lady Emma Teagle, died peacefully in her garden one warm June morning in 1955. Osborne told me she had been cutting roses to put in the silver bowl on the hall table. The doctor said her heart had packed up. I was not surprised for she had given much of it away throughout her long and interesting life.

It fell upon me to go through the study she and my father had shared before he died. Sorting out their papers was a slow business. I kept our letters from school which she had carefully put in date order and tied up with blue ribbons, along with our school reports, and letters from my father to her.

Opening yet another drawer, I found it full of letters – from a Dutch couple, a boy called Samuel da Souza, and a Cornish farmer. Four of my mother's diaries were also in that drawer.

I had not realised how greatly affected my parents were by the arrival of an old Dutch paddle-steamer full of Jewish refugees. That was in May 1940 when my father, Admiral Sir `William Teagle was Commander-in-Chief Nore, based in Chatham and responsible for naval operational control of the southern North Sea area from the Thames Estuary to the Humber. Nor had I realised they had stayed in touch with a few of them all their lives, even though mother had mentioned the paddle-boat, *De Ruyter,* in one or two letters to me. I knew all about 'engineer's tea' because my father drank it every day from the stained and battered tin mug I inherited.

I carried that drawer into the sitting room, placed it on a small table next to an armchair, opened the first letter and entered an unknown world.

Peter Teagle
October 1955

Chapter 1.

Cornwall – June 1940

"It is very quiet here," Jannie remarked after supper.

"Not really," their hostess, Miss Hartley, replied. "There's the mine in the valley and three flights a day from the aerodrome."

"Where to?" piped up Sam, who had never seen an aeroplane close up.

"To the Scillies. They often fly right over us."

As Sam's eyes lit up, Miriam interrupted. "Jannie, why don't you and Sam go for a walk? Betty and I will do the washing up."

It was their first night in Cornwall and Mimi did not want Sam reminded of the aircraft that bombed *De Ruyter*, killing Henri and so many others. She also wanted to ask her friend a few questions.

The evening was warm and just light enough to be able to walk easily along the track leading to the cliff edge. When they had a clear view of the sea, Jannie stopped to point out the dark shapes of a small convoy making its way to the north. "No lighthouses to help them," he commented.

"Does it ever get really dark?" asked Sam as he looked around.

Jannie laughed. "Oh yes. It's nearly midsummer now. There will be nights so dark we can't see our noses, and thick fogs too."

Sam shivered. "I think there are many ghosts here. In the house too."

Jannie ruffled the boy's hair. "Nee, jonge. That is just because it is all new to us."

He would not admit that he too felt there was a strange atmosphere in the house, and out here. Taking a cigar from his pocket, he turned his back to the sea, cupped his hands to shade the match and lit it. Before Sam could ask, Jannie said, "I learnt that years ago." He took the cigar from his mouth and held it so the lighted end was shielded by the palm of his hand. "From sailors who weren't supposed to smoke on watch." Sighing, he looked at the boy. "And now it is wartime I do it here."

When they were alone, Miriam put her tea-towel down and said, "We must talk, Betty. I'll put the kettle on."

They took the tray into the sitting room and sat in the half-darkness where Mimi lit a cigarette. After a long silence she said, "I am worried about Sam. That boy has been through too much." She looked out of the window. "He's escaped, but his family hasn't. He insisted on going to Dunkirk with the men. And…" she took a deep drag at her cigarette. "And they insisted on taking him."

Looking at Betty, she spat out, "Duty, they said! They must do their duty. How many men die doing their duty." A tear glistened on her cheek. "Henri. Dirk too. They had done their duty getting to England. The Navy could have sailed that ship but no, they went for the honour of Holland."

Mimi sighed. "I'm sorry, my dear. I had to get that off my chest."

Betty was silent for a long time before asking, "What do you hope for down here?"

"I really do not know." She looked across the dark room. "It was important to get out of London before the Germans start bombing it. Sam needs to be kept busy to stop him brooding. Jannie is most insistent about that and he is right. We think working on a farm would suit him, but what do we know?"

Betty saw her shoulders slump. "Jannie is right," she said brightly. "I know a lot more about farming than I did at the beginning of the war." She laughed. "The Trevassos run a small farm and need a strong lad. They are kind, hard-working and decent people. I would not have recommended them otherwise. If they like Sam he will be made welcome and given work. They will show him what to do and," she paused, "And I think their dog will soon be having puppies."

Miriam laughed. "That is what Henk said he needed." Sensing Betty's question, she explained, "Another Dutch sailor, now living on a farm in Hampshire. He and a Jewish woman seem to have adopted a little girl and the farmer gave her a puppy." Suddenly serious, she said quietly, "She is three. Her parents put her on the boat and left her there." Hearing Betty's gasp, she went on quickly. "They had no choice. They stayed behind to look after aged parents."

Betty shook her head. "We know nothing of war, not yet." She went to the window and looked out. "I work on a farm with other girls. Farmers need us to replace the boys who have joined the Army and we do a good job. Sam is needed on the farm here and will do a good job in time. But what about you, Miriam, what will you and Jannie do?"

Miriam sighed deeply. "That is what I really wanted to talk to you about." She sighed again. "What will we do? What is there to do once Sam is working every day?" She got up to stand beside Betty and said, almost to herself, "Jannie needs to keep busy, almost more than Sam." She choked back a sob. "His closest friend died in his arms. What does that do to a man?"

Betty took her arm. "What do you want to do, my dear? What do you do best?"

Miriam turned to face her, straightening her back as she did. "What I want to do, my friend, and what I have to do, are different. Right now, I have to stay here to make sure Sam is safe. So does Jannie. When we are sure he is settled, when he is sleeping without nightmares, when the farmer tells us he wants to keep Sam on, then we may think about ourselves."

"But what do you do best?" Betty was persistent.

Miriam was silent for a long time. What she had done best died with her children. She shook her head, as if not wishing to reply. "What I do is look after people who live near me in London. Some are old, some young, some not able to work, some young mothers; all are poor. I am not poor, Betty, and I am able to help in many small ways. I thought I could leave them when I came down here. I thought I could look after

Sam and help Jannie. But I cannot." She sighed. "Jannie should come back to London with me. He will want to stay close to Sam, but I do not think that will be good for either of them. Not once Sam has settled to life on the farm. I hope he will be able to live with this family and that he will find comfort through hard work and their kindness."

Betty laughed. "I did not tell you they have a daughter, Annie, and she is much the same age as Sam. I think they might well become friends."

Miriam smiled, the blackness lifting from her thoughts. "That is the best news I have heard for days."

Sam was mesmerised by the great arc of stars hanging over them in the vast velvet sky. "Oh Jannie," he whispered, "have you ever seen anything like this?"

Jannie smiled. "We cannot see stars in the city, Sam, but they are always there. It is just as dark where Oom Paul lives. Your parents could be standing in his farmyard and looking at them right now." He put his hand on the lad's shoulder. "When I was a boy and a long way from home, I went on deck at night, looked up at the stars, and sent messages to my Mutti and Papa." He gave Sam a gentle nudge, "Why don't you talk to them now?" Not waiting for an answer, he moved a few paces away. "I'll wait here."

Sam closed his eyes and took a deep breath. He saw his parents, he saw Rachel, heard their voices, felt a quiet peace envelop him and raised his eyes to the heavens.

Sam stirred after a few minutes and sought Jannie. "Danke," he whispered, "let us go back now."

Chapter 2.

Sam insisted on opening the bedroom curtains once Jannie had blown out their candle. He lay on his side, gazing at the stars and listening to the music of the stream chuckling its way through the valley below.

When Jannie heard the boy's quiet, even breathing he rolled over and closed his eyes. It was the first time Sam had not cried himself to sleep since they came ashore.

Breakfast over, chores completed, boots polished and uniforms brushed down, Jannie and Sam went outside to wait for Tante Mimi and Miss Hartley.

"Remember, jonge, you must look Meneer Trevasso in the eyes when answering. And don't fidget when he's talking."

"Oh Jannie, you've told me this already." Sam kicked at the grass. "And I shall tell him the truth. And what Papa told me to say." Sam looked at the old engineer, "It was better on board …" and suddenly stopped, his eyes filling as memories of their last voyage came flooding back.

Jannie stood still as Sam took a shuddering breath, his face set and grim, while those same memories swept through him. Such was the pain that he did not trust himself to speak.

Miriam came outside, saw their faces and walked quietly up to the men she loved. Taking Sam's hand in hers, she drew him to her side even as she reached for Jannie. "Come, my dears," she whispered, "We must go. Betty will catch us up."

"Danke," said Jannie, squeezing her hand before tucking her arm under his. Sam kept hold as they set off, only letting go when Miss Hartley came striding along behind them.

"Well," she said brightly, "This is an adventure."

Nanjigga Farm crouched on the side of a hill sloping down to the sea, a small, granite building surrounded by granite barns, with high stone walls enclosing the yard and kitchen garden.

"It must be tough here when the wind's blowing," muttered Jannie before tapping Betty on the arm. "Please, mevrouw, one minute." They stopped on the track a few paces from the front door.

He and Miriam looked Sam up and down. "Polish your boots, jonge." When Sam had rubbed one and then the other against his trouser legs, Mimi spat on her handkerchief and wiped a smear from his cheek. Recoiling, Sam choked out "That's what Mutti did."

"Forgive me," she whispered, kissing Sam's forehead. "I haven't done that for twenty years."

Betty greeted Mrs Trevasso warmly before introducing Miriam, Jannie and Sam.

"Come in my dears," said Mrs T. "Come and meet my husband." Seeing Sam's worried expression, she smiled at him, "Don't worry, he won't bite."

Mr Trevasso rose as they came in, noting the way the old man and boy stood close together and how they looked quickly around the room. Introductions made, he sat Jannie and Sam opposite himself, with the two women at each end of the table.

The door to the yard banged open. "Dad…!" Annie came dancing into the parlour, eyes gleaming with excitement. She was bursting with the thrill of her gallop across the fields on Janet, their chestnut mare, and itching to tell her father they had jumped the new five-bar gate into the field.

She stopped, staring at the two men in unusual uniforms and the neat suit of the elegant older woman. Only Miss Hartley was familiar.

"Hello honey," smiled Miss Hartley. "Did you enjoy your ride?"

"Oh yes, Miss H. It was …"

"Tell us later, Annie," interrupted Mr T. "Come and meet our guests." He patted the empty chair beside him.

Annie sat down and looked more closely at the strangers. The men, no, one man and a boy, were obviously foreign, sailors she guessed. The woman could be English and definitely lived in a city. They all looked awkward and out of place, especially the boy. She wondered why he was staring at her.

Sam had never seen a girl wearing trousers, nor one in a shirt streaked with sweat, nor one so brown, radiating good health, curiosity and humour sparkling in her clear grey eyes.

"Annie." He rolled her name around beneath his breath and only stopped staring when he heard Mis Hartley say "…and this is Sam."

"And Sam is why we are here," Tante Mimi said, addressing Mr Trevasso. "Miss Hartley has told us you might like help on the farm." She looked fondly at Sam. "He is a good boy and a hard worker."

"Ja," Jannie confirmed, breaking his awkward silence, "Very good worker."

Mr T gazed at the boy. Miss Hartley had told him Sam was sixteen and had been a sailor, but he was much younger than that. He thought a boy that pale and skinny could not have been much of a sailor and doubted he would be any use on the farm. He sucked contemplatively on his pipe before saying, "Show me your hands, boy."

Jannie nodded at Sam and growled, "It's alright jonge."

Sam stood, conscious of everyone staring at him, squared his shoulders and walked round the table to the farmer. Bowing slightly, he held out his right hand.

Mr T took it in his own large brown hand and shook it. He was surprised by the strength of Sam's grip. He was even more surprised when he turned it over to examine the calluses he had felt, and saw that Sam's palm and fingers were ingrained with dirt. His left hand was the same.

Sam laughed when he saw his expression. "I am an engineer, meneer. It is not possible to have clean hands."

Jannie said nothing.

Mimi had seen the sudden interest in Annie's eyes and was beginning to wonder if it was wise to leave Sam on the farm.

Mrs T had also seen Annie's interest and wondered the same.

Mr T admired Sam's spirit and thought he would like to have him on the farm, as long as he was a quick learner.

Annie was intrigued.

"Well, Sam," replied Mr Trevasso, "We don't have much use for engineers on the farm." He sensed Sam stiffen. Going on in his slow, measured way, he added, "However, if you can shovel coal all day there is much to be shovelled on the farm." His eyes twinkled. "Much else to do too, if you are willing to learn."

Sam studied the man before him. He looked kind. He turned towards Mrs Trevasso. "I can also cook, mevrouw, and make tea and coffee." He looked to Jannie for confirmation. "We sailors are very clean and wash our own clothes. My mother…" Abruptly he stopped, his face suddenly gaunt. Taking a deep breath, he continued, "My mother taught me many things." He sat down, staring at the table.

Annie shivered. The room felt cold. It was the first time she had seen the face of war.

Mrs T rose to her feet. "Come Sam, we'll make a pot of tea."

Annie saw her father smiling to himself and knew he would take the boy on. She wondered how long Sam would last.

Chapter 3.

After a quick lunch, Betty announced, "I have to go back to work today. I had hoped for another day off, but I've had a letter asking me to come straightaway."

"What do you do?" Jannie did not know about the Women's Land Army; Betty enlightened him.

"Hard work," he mused.

"Very," laughed Betty, "I'll be away for a couple of weeks." Sensing their concern, she added, "Jim Semmens knows the house well. He'll help if you have any problems."

With that she stood up, patted Mimi on the back and left.

Fortunately, she had told Miriam what shops there were and that there was a bank in the little town, as well as a post office and police house. While Sam washed up, Mimi and Jannie made a list. Miriam loved lists. Mr T had told them what the boy needed, and that Sam should wear his boots to work. They did not have to buy much, just one shirt, some vests and another pair of dungarees. Mr T explained they had oilskins and gumboots that should fit and not to buy too much, as Sam was a growing boy.

Having registered their arrival at the police house and finished their shopping, they walked back to their new home. "Let's go exploring." Jannie had found a map in the bookcase and laid it flat on the table. "We are here," putting his finger on the map. "Here is the valley and there is the sea. It's not far."

A sudden, muffled explosion shook the house, rattling crockery, windows and doors. Terrified, Sam ran outside.

Jannie froze. He closed his eyes and took a deep breath, trying to dispel the fear that gripped his stomach.

"What on earth…? Anxious and frightened, Miriam turned to Jannie. She was appalled to see him trembling, his face white and his eyes tightly closed. As she reached for his hand, he shook himself, opened his eyes and looked at her. "Too many ghosts," he whispered. "Where's Sam?"

They found him outside. "What was that?" Sam's voice quavered.

There were no aeroplanes about, no ships to be seen. Just machinery working in the valley below them. Jannie relaxed when he remembered they were in mining country. It must have been blasting, deep underground.

"Let's ask Jim," he suggested quietly. "I don't think it's anything to worry about."

It was as Jannie thought. Most afternoons, except Saturdays and Sundays, the miners blasted the rock they had been drilling that day and then went home while the dust settled.

Jim also told them that, as the valley was busy during the day, visitors were not welcome.

They walked home, wondering what other surprises might be in store for them.

***

Sam's tears returned that night. Mimi and Jannie were talking quietly in the kitchen when Jannie held up his hand. Mimi saw him cock his head towards the open door before she too heard Sam's muffled sob.

"That poor boy," she whispered. "Shall I go to him?"

Jannie shook his head. "Nee, my dear, leave him for a minute or two." He poured them both another brandy and lit a cigarette. "Perhaps that explosion gave him a nachtmerrie." He asked, "How d'you say that in English?"

"Nightmare." Mimi helped herself to a cigarette, thinking, *Jannie must be worried, to forget his manners.* She reached for his hand and shook it lightly. "I'm surprised you don't have them."

Jannie looked at Miriam, his face bleak, and whispered, "I do."

Feeling him trembling again, Miriam put her hands behind his head and drew it to her breast. "You poor dear man," she said, her voice soft as she stroked his neck, "You poor, dear, kind man." She felt the tension in his shoulders and massaged them gently, all the while rocking him to and fro, as if he were a child.

After a while Jannie put his arms around Miriam, pulled her closer and ran his fingers up and down her spine. She gave a little gasp, kissed the top of his head and whispered, "Perhaps we had better stop."

Leaning back, Jannie smiled at her and asked, "Why?" before kissing the inside of her wrist. "You are even more beautiful when you go pink."

Miriam pushed him away as he stood up. "And you are a very naughty man."

They jumped as Sam pushed the door open and asked, "Why is Jannie naughty?"

He gazed at them sleepily, dried tears still on his cheeks.

Miriam was first to respond. "Because he tells me stories."

Sam nodded and came further into the kitchen. He looked at Jannie, "That bang." He gulped, "It was like the bomb," and burst into tears. Jannie wrapped his arms around the boy and pulled him to his chest.

"Not so noisy," he whispered, ruffling Sam's hair. "But it made all of us jump." He put a hand under Sam's chin and gently lifted it. "Did you see how high Mimi went?"

Sam nodded. "Nearly as high as you."

Mimi laughed. "Shall I put the kettle on?"

Chapter 4.

"It's time to go." Jannie was waiting by the back door with Sam's knapsack. "You don't want to be late on your first day."

Sam put on his jacket and cap, hugged Mimi and walked slowly out of the house.

"Nervous, jonge?"

Sam nodded. "Why do I have to go?"

Jannie looked at him. "You know why. They need a strong young lad on the farm, not an old man like me." He kicked a stone along the track. "Someone has to work, or we'll soon run out of money."

They walked on in silence until Jannie stopped to light a cigar. "I don't have many left," he said sadly. "I should have bought more from your papa."

Sam looked at him. "I never saw you there."

"That's because you were at school or on the quay. I used to go once a week, mid-morning when we were on the Hoek run." He nudged Sam, "Of course, that stopped when you came onboard.

"Why?" asked Sam, intrigued.

"I had you to train, jonge. I couldn't leave you alone in the engine room, could I?"

Sam laughed. "I learn quickly, don't I?" He was ever so proud of being rated Engineer Second Class.

"Indeed you do," Jannie replied fondly. "And you will learn to be a farmer even faster."

Sam scowled at him and walked on.

Mr Trevasso met them at the farmyard gate. "Morning Sam. Morning Jannie." He led them across the yard to the back door of the farm house. "Come on in. We've just finished breakfast."

Mrs T sat them at the table and poured two mugs of tea. "When you've finished that, Sam, Annie will show you round the farm. She'll be here in a minute."

Once the young people had gone, Jannie was not surprised when Mr T suggested he might like to look around with him.

Leaning on a gate overlooking the cove below, Jannie turned to Frank Trevasso. "You have a good place here, but it must be hard work."

"Very." They both lit up, taciturn, hard-working men who conserved words as carefully as they conserved energy.

"Sam will learn quickly."

Frank nodded. "Annie will teach him." He looked at Jannie, "I hope he behaves himself."

Jannie laughed, "He's too young for …" He stopped abruptly, cursing his loose tongue.

Frank looked steadily at Jannie. "I guessed as much. How old is he?"

"His papers say he is sixteen…"

"Never mind what they say. How old is he?"

Jannie paused, took a long drag on his cigarette, exhaled and replied, "He is fourteen; and a Jew." Frank raised an eyebrow. "His father got him false papers, got them for the whole family." He looked at the farmer. "It is difficult for Jews to get into England."

They were silent for several minutes. Eventually Frank stirred. "He's welcome here, Jannie. We have enough work to keep him busy."

Jannie gave a brief nod. "He needs to be kept busy. That is why we left London. There is not much for him to do there. He needs to be kept so busy he is too tired to think."

Straightening and turning to face the farmer, he told him, "That boy has seen too much, been through too much. He needs time and hard work,-kindness and…" He stopped, his voice breaking, "…and love. He needs to be loved."

"What happened, Jannie?"

Jannie stared out to sea for a long time, his shoulders slumped. Frank noticed his hands were trembling and remained silent. Eventually Jannie gripped the top bar of the gate with both hands, his knuckles white. He pushed himself away and looked at the farmer.

Never had Frank seen such lines etched into a man's face. His lips were compressed, a muscle working in his cheek; his eyes, sunk into his skull, were glistening with unshed tears. "We were bombed, that is what happened." He sighed and closed his eyes. Frank had to bend his head to hear what Jannie said. "Bombed and shot at on our way back from Dunkirk." There was another long silence before he continued in that same soft, low monotone. "Many were killed. My friend …" He brushed away a tear, "My friend Henri was wounded."

He stopped again, shook his head, opened his eyes and straightened up. "He bled to death in my arms."

Jannie gripped Frank's arm, "We went to war, meneer. That is what happened, and that is why we are here."

Panting a little, he let go of Frank's arm. "You have to keep him busy, so busy he cannot think, make him so tired he sleeps without dreams."

Frank nodded slowly, his eyes never leaving Jannie's gaunt face. "And what about you, Jannie? What will you do?"

Chapter 5.

"What will I do?" Jannie sighed. "I do not know." He looked at Frank. "That is, apart from making sure Sam is safe. We promised to do that."

Frank took his pipe out of his mouth. "Sam will be safe here. There is much for him to do, much for us all. I expect he will struggle to start with." He laughed. "He has to prove to me that he can stick to the task he's given and do it properly. I can't take on anyone who needs much supervision."

Jannie nodded. "That is how I started him. Cleaning out the ash. It's a filthy job."

"So is cleaning out the pig house," Frank remarked dryly. "And I have a plot of land that needs digging." He looked at Jannie. "If he gets here on time, works hard and fits in with us this coming week, I think he should move in with us."

Jannie raised an eyebrow.

"We start early and finish late. It's better if farm hands live on the farm." He smiled, "We have room in the house.

There was a long silence. Jannie had thought it would be a few weeks before Sam was ready for this.

He sighed. "It would be better for Sam. I wonder what he will say." He glanced at Frank, "Should that come from you or me?"

"Me," Frank replied without hesitation. "It is common practice." He noticed Jannie grimace as he turned away. "Listen, Jannie." He waited until the older man was facing him. "We will look after that boy as if he was our own son. He will work hard, but no harder than Annie. Our farm is a happy place." He paused, suddenly remembering what Miss Hartley had told him. "And Breeze is about to have puppies." He laughed. "My dog. She's called Breeze. I gather you think he might like one."

Jannie's face lightened. "That is true. Miriam and I discussed this in London. It will be very special for him. Make him forget this verdomd war."

"Which," said Frank, "brings me back to you." He filled his pipe and lit it, studying Jannie as he did so. "What will *you* do to forget the war?"

Jannie stared out to sea where a small convoy was making its way round Land's End, knowing he would never again go to sea. Turning his back on the ocean, he put into words for the first time what he had been thinking for many days.

"If Sam is settled and happy on the farm, I will go back to London with Miriam." He shrugged. "It will be difficult for me and for Sam, but better for both of us." He lit a cigarette. "Miriam has much to do in London and I will help her. She would stay here if Sam needed her, as would I, but I do not think two old people fussing around will be good for Sam – or you. Nor would it be good for us."

Frank put a hand on Jannie's shoulder. "True enough, and hard to say. Harder still to do. But it will be better for Sam."

Chapter 6.

"Well," said Mimi, as the pony and trap clattered down the lane after taking Sam and his bags to his new home, "The house is going to seem very empty."

"Yes," Jannie agreed, "And we must keep busy."

They went inside, closed the door and sat at the table, smoking. Presently Mimi fetched a bottle of Armagnac and two glasses. "A toast," she said brightly, "to Sam." And burst into tears.

Taking the glass from her, Jannie said quietly, "We know this is best for the boy."

Mimi nodded, dried her eyes and smiled at him. "But not so good for us." They laughed and stood to clear away the tea things.

Later that evening they walked out to the White Gate and sat on the stile, smoking and talking quietly, conscious of looks from the locals out for their Sunday evening stroll. "I'm glad we got the flags sewn onto our uniforms," Jannie remarked, "otherwise I'd be marched off at the end of a pitch fork."

"It's not surprising they're edgy," Mimi said. "The wireless is full of warnings about strangers."

Jannie laughed, "I am glad I'm not a nun!" They had heard stories about German parachutists disguising themselves as nuns. "Imagine floating down with your habit round your neck."

Chuckling, they left, casting a lingering look at the farm below as they made their way back to the Count House.

Miriam was aware how awkward Jannie felt. She smiled; *How kind and gentle he is; I wonder what he is thinking?* She had noticed how quickly he stood back once she had dried her eyes, how he made sure his hands did not brush against hers and wished… she cut that thought short, not knowing what she wished.

The subject of her thoughts was in turmoil. He walked slowly by her side, a decent gap between them, her faint scent tantalising his senses. With Sam gone, Jannie was purposeless for the first time in his life. He ran through his conversation with Mr Trevasso, how he told him he would go back to London to look after Mimi, but what if she did not want him there, or told him he should stay here in case Sam needed him? The easy intimacy they had shared when Sam was present, had left with him.

Jannie lit the candles they had left on the kitchen table and handed one to Mimi. Awkwardly he muttered, "I'll use the bathroom first and get to bed."

Mimi smiled at his solemn expression, "Thank you, Jannie. Good night my dear."

It was a warm, quiet night. Jannie blew out the candle and opened the blackout curtains to let in the breeze. He sat on the edge of Sam's bed, smoking a last cigarette, and then turned in. After a while he heard Miriam's door close and wondered what she had been doing. As he drifted off Jannie was conscious of Sam's empty bed and a new and unwelcome distance between him and Mimi.

It must have been an hour later that Miriam was woken by a muffled sound coming from the adjacent room. She frowned. Perhaps she was dreaming? Then she heard a groan. Propping herself on one elbow, she reached for the matches to light her candle. There it was again. Slipping out of bed, she pulled on her house-robe and opened the door. Jannie's breathing was loud, ragged and interspersed with groans

Thinking he was in pain, Miriam went into his room and tiptoed to the side of his bed. There was enough light for her to see that his eyes were tightly closed and his forehead beaded with sweat. She leaned over to wake him. Suddenly Jannie grabbed her throat, snarling as he squeezed and shook her.

"Jannie," she gasped. "Stop! Jannie, stop. It's me."

His eyes flicked opened, wild, staring without seeing. His hands slackened. Wrenching herself out of his grasp. Mimi stepped away, shaking, fearful lest he leap at her.

Jannie lay still, panting, his eyes closed. Mimi watched as his breathing slowed, saw his eyes open, his head move to look around the room, his surprise at seeing her.

"What are you doing here?" he croaked.

"I thought you were ill," Mimi whispered, "You were groaning." Struggling to compose herself, she continued, "And then ...then you attacked me..." Her voice shook. "I was so frightened." Trembling, tears flowing down her cheeks, she closed her eyes to block out the experience.

Appalled, Jannie got out of bed and put his arms around her. Mimi gasped and tried to push him away, whimpering. "Don't hurt me, Jannie. I beg you. Don't hurt me."

"Nee, my love, I would never hurt you. Never." He stroked her hair away from her face. "Hush, Mimi, hush my dear." He pulled her gently to him, her head on his shoulder, gently rubbing her back as he whispered, "It was a bad dream."

Gradually Miriam's heart stopped racing, her body ceased trembling. Suddenly conscious of Jannie's arms around her, the stubble on his chin against her cheek, the warmth of his body against hers, she tensed as if to pull away. When Jannie eased his arms to let her go, fear was replaced by a wave of comfort that swept through her. Putting her hands on his cheeks, she drew his face to hers and kissed him.

Chapter 7.

Mr T had suggested that Miriam and Jannie let Sam settle in before they visited him. Much as they wanted to see him, they kept away from the farm. There were a few odd jobs that needed doing at the Count House, but never enough to keep them busy.

They spent days spent walking on the moors or along the cliff-top paths, sandwiches and hard-boiled eggs in a knapsack and a flask of cold tea to quench their thirst. The sun shone brighter, the sea was bluer and the air warmer and softer than ever either of them had thought possible.

There always seemed to be a rock to climb where a steadying hand was needed or a path easier to walk when hand in hand. Preparing and cooking meals was quicker done together, sometimes chattering away like sparrows, at other times in contented silence.

Evenings were their favourite time of day; a stroll to the White Gate, followed by a glass or two of brandy on the big sofa in the sitting room, Jannie propped up in one corner with Mimi stretched out beside him, her head on his thigh, his hand in hers.

They were supremely happy.

One evening, Jannie kissed the top of Mimi's head and asked, "Do you want to go back to London?"

She looked up to study his face. "Why do you ask?"

"What are we doing here?" He stroked her cheek. "If Sam has settled in, he will be safe here. The Trevassos will look after him and he will always be busy." He stared into space for a while before shifting. Mimi sat up.

So quietly that she had to strain to hear his words, he explained, "That evening I nearly killed you." He stopped, looked at her and shook his head. "I thought you were taking Henri from me. As long as I held him he lived."

She felt him trembling and took his hands in hers. "Do you often get this dream?"

He sighed. "It is not a dream. I smell his blood, feel his breath, his heart's faint beat." Jannie turned to look at Mimi. "I miss him every day. Night is worse."

His face lit up with a joyful smile. "But not now, mijn liefie. Not with you."

He stood, stretched, lit two cigarettes and passed one to Mimi. "I think you must go back to London."

Inhaling deeply, he held the smoke in his lungs before continuing. "Your work…" He looked at Mimi. "Your work is important. You have people who need you. I would like to come with you. I need to be busy, so busy I am too tired to dream."

He held up his hand as Mimi started to speak. "That is not all, my dear." He smiled wickedly. "What would Miss Hartley say if she found us in bed tog…"

Miriam cut him off with a well-aimed cushion.

Chapter 8.

"Did you draw this?" Miriam was looking at a sketch of a paddle-steamer she found when tidying the sitting-room.

"Ja," Jannie looked embarrassed. "It's not so good."

"Don't be silly. It's lovely." Mimi studied it more closely. "Where did you learn to draw?"

"At sea." Jannie laughed. "Some made model ships, or sewed, or embroidered, or wrote. Fancy rope-work was popular. Others drew and painted pictures." He took the drawing from her. "I haven't picked up a pencil or paint brush for a long time, my dear. Not for a very long time." He held the paper up to the light and sighed. "She did not look like this when we left her."

"Oh Jannie." Mimi put her arm round his waist. "I wish I could draw like you." She leaned her head against his shoulder. "Would you draw more pictures? Show me what *De Ruyter* was like, where you and Sam worked, what you did?" She looked at him. "I know so little about you, dear man."

Jannie laughed, put his sketch down and embraced her. "I will do this for you, my love. Of course I will."

Having found and dusted off a couple of deck-chairs, Jannie and Miriam took to sitting in the south-facing back garden in the late afternoon sun. While Jannie drew, Mimi wrote. She was preparing for their return to London.

They were to look back on their time in Cornwall as a time of great tranquillity, a rare and precious moment of peace amidst the brutal chaos of war.

"Is that someone at the door?" Mimi got up and walked across the grass.

"Oh, hello," she called to Mr and Mrs Trevasso. "We're in the garden."

Jannie set out two more deck-chairs and a small table while Mimi made a pot of tea.

"I expect you'd like to know how Sam is." Mrs T had waited until they were all seated. "He's certainly a quick learner."

"And a hard worker," interjected Mr T, "Just as you said."

"But does he talk to you?" asked Mimi. "Does he join in?"

"He didn't at first," Mr T replied, looking to his wife for confirmation. "He was quiet, withdrawn, as you would expect."

"He didn't wet his bed," Mrs T added, "just his pillow."

"Oh Sam," breathed Mimi. "You poor boy."

"It took him a day or two," Mrs T continued, "before he started asking questions. We asked Annie to help him."

"And gave them a filthy job to do last week," said Mr T. "You would have been impressed." This to Jannie. "Sifting the ash out of an old bonfire. That broke the ice."

Mrs T saw the concern on Miriam's face and patted her arm. "They were covered in ash from head to toe." She laughed. "They washed it off in the sea, changed into clean clothes and were back in time for milking."

"I should like to have seen that." Jannie laughed. "Are they talking to each other?"

"Oh yes," said Mrs T. "Annie can be a bit stand-offish, being an only child, but she is looking after Sam in her own way."

"And is Sam responding?" Mimi wondered what Mrs T meant. "Is he talking to her?"

"Yes." Mr T fielded her question. "Not about his home, not yet, and Annie doesn't ask him. They talk about the farm and their work, animals and why we do certain things. Sam is very curious and Annie is a patient and thorough teacher."

"That was a surprise," added Mrs T. "A very pleasant surprise." She looked at Miriam. "We hadn't seen that side of her before."

Relaxing, Miriam looked at Jannie before asking them, "Will you be keeping him on?"

"Lord yes," replied Mr T without hesitation. "He has the makings of being the best lad we've had on the farm."

"And he's good about the house," Mrs T said, "considerate and very clean, just like he told us, and wonderful manners. You don't see manners like that these days."

"Does he miss us much?" Mimi asked quietly.

Mr T cocked his head to one side and looked from Miriam to Jannie. "He does not have time to, Mrs Cohen." He paused. "He works hard all day and sleeps well at night. There were tears to begin with, as Martha said. But not after the first few days."

Relieved, Miriam refilled their cups and offered her cigarettes around.

"How about you two?" asked Mr T. "Do you miss him?"

"Oh yes." Mimi and Jannie said together.

"I miss him terribly," Mimi whispered, "But he must stay with you." She stopped. "If you really meant what you said about him being a good worker."

"And you, Jannie?"

Jannie looked at the farmer, saw the concern and understanding in his eyes and replied. "I miss him, meneer, as much as Miriam does. Of course I do. But Sam is in the best possible place. If you can keep him busy, if he is being useful and feels welcome in your home, then he should stay with you."

"Well," said Mr T. "That is clear enough. Sam stays with us and we will look after him as if he were our own son."

He looked again at Miriam and asked, "When will you go back to London?"

"When Sam has a puppy."

Chapter 9.

Jannie and Miriam walked with the Trevassos as far as the White Gate where Mr T gave his wife and Miriam a hand to climb over the granite hedge.

The two men lit their pipes and walked slowly down the track to a bench overlooking the cove. Once settled, Mr T asked, "What is troubling you?"

Jannie was silent for a while. He was asking himself the same question. Eventually he replied, "I vowed I would keep Sam safe when we buried Henri. I swore that as his body sank into the depths." He closed his eyes, picturing the swirl in the green water, the string of bubbles rising and dissolving, hearing again the hiss of steam escaping from the shot-up funnel, feeling Sam's hand in his.

"I have no children, meneer. No ties, not then. Now I have Sam." He smiled a little as he said, "And Miriam…

"Henri was my friend. For twenty years we worked together. We lived close to each other and were content. The river was enough, the ship our real home." His face hardened as he went on. "We knew the Germans would come. There were people in Holland who believed in what Hitler was doing. They were Fascists, Nazis, wicked people. A poison was spreading across the country. Not as bad as in Germany, but bad enough."

Sitting on that bench as the sun went down, he told Mr T what it was like to live in a country on the edge of war, a country powerless to resist invasion by its neighbour, the growing fears of their Jewish friends, the steady influx of Jewish and other refugees from Germany, the vile rise of antisemitism that drove Sam's family to place him onboard *De Ruyter*, how his family were unable to escape when the Germans invaded.

Mr T had never seen a face so harrowed by sorrow as when Jannie turned to tell him about their escape and why they went to Dunkirk.

"You understand, meneer, I love that boy as if he was my own?"

Mr T nodded.

"You understand why he must be kept busy?"

Mt T nodded again.

"So must I, meneer. So must I." Jannie sighed. "I must work, and that work is in London. With Miriam." He looked at the farmer. "She was helping many people before we came away. She must return to help them again. And I will go with her." He sighed. "I do not want to leave Sam, but he is safe here." He paused. "It will not be safe in London. Not when they start bombing." He stared out to sea. "I have my duty to Sam and now I have my duty to Miriam."

Jannie shivered, as if a chill wind was blowing. "What will Sam say when I tell him?"

"Sam will be sad, but not for long," Frank reassured him. "He does not have time to think as there is always so much to do." He chuckled. "Every day is different and Sam has much to learn."

"I wonder where they are?" Martha was surprised that neither Annie nor Sam was anywhere to be seen. She had expected Annie would have seen them coming and put the kettle on. It was unlike her to be away from the house when her parents went out.

Miriam touched her arm. "Look."

Sam was backing out of a barn holding something to his chest, closely followed by a smiling Annie. Seeing her mother and Mimi, she skipped across the yard. "Breeze has had her puppies." Pointing to Sam, she said, "Come and see the one he's chosen."

Having admired Sam's puppy, Martha insisted he put her back in the stable, checked the rest of the litter and patted Breeze. "Clever girl," she said, closing the stable door.

When Jannie and Frank inspected the litter, Frank murmured, "Sam has his puppy."

Chapter 10.

Mimi and Jannie walked slowly up to the Carne in the deepening twilight. As no-one else was there, Jannie put his arms around Mimi and hugged her. She leant against him, welcoming the warmth and security of his embrace, placing one hand upon his neck and the other in the small of his back.

They stood silent and still for several minutes until Mimi raised her head. She kissed Jannie lightly on the cheek and whispered, "Sam has his puppy."

Jannie nodded, looking at her. "Yes, my dear, and I have a question."

Letting go of Mimi, he stood back slightly, the better to see her. Puzzled, Mimi waited, a faint smile on her lips, wondering what surprise he had in store for her.

"Where will I live when we go back to London?"

She had not expected that. "Why, with me, of course."

"Hmm. And what about your reputation, mevrouw?"

Mimi had not thought of this. "Pff. A fig for my reputation."

Jannie did not move. "You cannot say that my dear. I too have my reputation. It is all I have."

Mimi said nothing. She had not thought of that either. Nor did she expect the next question.

Taking her hands in his, Jannie gazed at Miriam for a moment before asking, "Will you marry me?"

"Of course I will."

With joy lighting up his face, Jannie picked her up, swung her round, kissed her. "Good." He kissed her again. "We will marry before we leave."

"Perhaps," said Jannie, as they strolled home by starlight, "Perhaps I should ask Sam if I may marry his aunt."

"If he was still living with us, I'm sure he'd think we are already married." Mimi squeezed Jannie's arm, "but I think he would like to be asked." Suddenly serious, she added, "And we must tell him we're going back to London."

"Ja," Jannie put his hand on hers, "in a day or two. There's no rush."

Jim dropped them off at the Town Hall, and told them where and when he would collect them.

It was another beautiful day, made better by the ease with which they were able to arrange their wedding. It seemed that a golden guinea could melt the heart of the iciest official. Taking Jim's advice, they soon found Simpsons where Jannie left Miriam to choose her wedding frock. He needed to find the jeweller's Jim had recommended and make a few other purchases.

They went back to the farm after milking, to have supper with the Trevassos.

"Nervous?"

Mimi laughed. "How did you know?"

"Because I am." Jannie touched her hand. "Sam won't bite us."

"No, my dear, but we might hurt him."

Jannie sighed, took her hand and said, "Let us give him a reason to be happy."

The chatter around the table died away as they walked hand-in-hand into the parlour. Sam was the first to react, bouncing from his chair, a broad smile lighting up his face. Looking from one to the other, he shouted, "Are you getting married?"

"Sam!" Mrs Trevasso admonished. Shaking her head, she smiled at the couple. "Ignore him, he has no manners."

Miriam laughed. "He has no manners," she agreed, glancing fondly at Jannie. "He is a ship's engineer, after all."

"Huh!" Jannie let go of Mimi's hand to pull Sam closer to them. "Do you think we should?"

"Of course." Squeaking with excitement, Sam wriggled free. "Are you?" He looked at Mimi.

"We are." And with that, congratulations, laughter and questions went tumbling around the room.

Chapter 11.

Sam's letter to my mother is typical of the many he wrote to her.

Milady,

Jannie and Tante Mimi were married yesterday. I was Jannie's best man and carried the wedding rings. Annie was Tante Mimi's maid of honour. Mr and Mrs Trevasso came, and Jim and Mrs Semmens, but Miss Hartley could not.

Jannie and I wore our uniforms. Tante Mimi wore a blue dress with little white dots and a straw hat with pale blue ribbon. She also wore your blue scarf and a gold necklace. She is very beautiful. Annie also wore a blue dress, the same as Tante Mimi. I did not know she had any dresses. Jannie stopped me saying anything. I told him I was only going to say she looked pretty, but Jannie did not believe me.

We had our photographs taken before going to a hotel for tea, where a band was playing. After tea Jannie and Mimi danced, then Mr and Mrs T. Annie asked me to dance. I don't know how to but Annie said it didn't matter as she'll teach me, as long as I don't tread on her toes. Thank goodness no-one looked at us.

Here is the wedding photo and one of Annie and me. She is the one in a frock (joke).

My puppy was very pleased to see us when we get back.

Your friend

Sam

"Good morning, Mevrouw Jansen." Jannie gazed into Mimi's soft, grey eyes, scarcely believing the truth of his words. She sat up and stretched out her hand to take the tea from him.

"Good morning, meneer," she smiled back at him. "Is it true? I thought I was dreaming."

"It is true." He shook his head in wonder. "And this is the first day of our married life." He laughed and waltzed around the room. Mimi put her cup down, drew back the covers and slid out of bed. Jannie paused in front of her, bowed and took her in his arms.

Eyes closed, cheek against cheek, they waltzed out of the bedroom, down the passage and into the sitting room where Jannie stopped, lifted her up and whirled her around. Breathless, laughing, they stood in the middle of the room, eyes still closed as they embraced.

When Jannie moved slightly to slide one hand down her back, Mimi opened her eyes, kissed the end of his nose and twisted free. Taking both his hands in hers, she whispered, "Later, my love. Today we have much to do."

That also was true, though most of the work was Mimi's once they had agreed what needed to be done.

Before anything could be decided, they had to tell her accountant, Harold Hartley, that they were coming back to London and ask him to make sure 17 Wilkes Street would be ready for them. Jannie had to notify the Dutch Embassy they were married and write to Lady Teagle and Henk.

With the nearest telephone over a mile away, it was easier to write letters; in between making lists of what they had to do, what they would need in London, talking about their future and sitting in the sun, holding hands and dreaming. All this was so tiring they had to lie down several times.

It was a day of many delights.

That evening, as they walked out to the cliff edge, Mimi asked, "Did you see Sam dancing with Annie?'

Jannie laughed. "Like a marionette!"

"Yes, but did you see his expression?" Jannie shook his head. He had only had eyes for Mimi.

"I think that must be the first time he has danced with a girl." Mimi smiled. "Annie will be a beauty when she is older."

Jannie looked at her, "Should we be worried about Sam?"

"No, my love. Frank and Martha may be worried later, but not now. Sam is too young and too busy to be thinking about girls." She laughed. "Except his favourite cow and his puppy."

A letter from Mr Hartley arrived two days later. Warmly congratulating Miriam on her marriage, he told her there would be no problems about moving back to Wilkes Street, asking only for a week's notice. He also enquired if her husband would be working upon his return.

It was time to talk to Sam about the future.

Frank saw them walking across the fields and went to meet them. "Well, my dears," he greeted them. "That was a grand day."

"It was indeed," replied Miriam. "Thank you for being our witnesses." She smiled at the farmer. "How are the young ones?"

"Back to normal, I'd say," Frank said. "Not sure Sam was too taken with the dancing." He laughed. "We'll have to teach him during the winter. Mrs T and I do love dancing."

"What about Annie?" Jannie was intrigued by the thought of Sam having dancing lessons in the farm-house. "Does she like dancing?"

"She's grown up with it," was all Mt T said as they reached the farmyard gate, where Sam spotted them and came running over.

"Come and see my puppy!" He tugged their hands and led them to the stable where Breeze and the puppies lived, just as Annie came out. She smiled shyly and went back with them.

Sam picked up one out of the wriggling, squeaking bundle. He looked at it carefully before handing it to Jannie. "This is Agathe."

As Jannie cradled her Mimi looked at Sam. "That's a lovely name…"

"Yes, Tante Mimi. We called our ship Agathe when we escaped. She kept us safe."

As Tante Mimi had not heard this story, Sam explained about the Swedish flag Willem and Dirk had stolen from the consulate in Rotterdam, fooling the Navy ship – and would have gone on talking if Frank had not interrupted him to remind him of his manners. Unabashed, Sam gave him a cheeky smile. "Sorry, m'baas," before asking, "would you like a cup of tea?" and adding as he led Mimi away, "We think Agathe was our English kapitein's girl-friend."

Jannie realised that Annie was hearing this story for the first time. He handed the puppy to her, saying quietly, "It is true, jonge, that is how we escaped."

Annie looked at him solemnly. "He doesn't tell me anything. Not really."

"One day he will tell you more," Jannie assured her. "He finds it easier not to at the moment." Choosing his words with care, he added, "He left his family behind and has seen too much of war." He stroked the puppy in her hands, "This little one will help him. And so will you."

"I will do my best."

"That is all anyone can do, my dear," Jannie replied, wishing, not for the first time, he had children of his own. He looked at the girl who would have to help Sam through the difficult days ahead.

"Listen, Annie, Miriam and I are going back to London soon." He stopped when he heard her gasp. "Sam will be upset when we tell him. I'm telling you now so you have a little time to think about what you can do."

"But why are you going?" Annie asked, close to tears. "I thought you liked it here."

"We do, Annie. We like it very much. But I need to be as busy as Sam. Old men also have bad dreams." He smiled at the girl. "In London, Miriam will be busy and I will be busy, too busy to dream."

"Oh," whispered Annie. "One day will you tell me what happened?"

"Yes," Jannie replied. "Of course." He straightened up. "Now we had better join the others."

Chapter 12.

"It's time we spoke to Sam."

It was three weeks before Miriam received a letter from Harold telling her Wilkes Street was empty. They could no longer put off breaking the news to Sam. "I'll go and ask Frank which morning we can come over."

They had agreed that it would be kindest to leave the same day, hard as that would be.

It was after milking the next day that Jannie and Miriam arrived at the farm. The Trevassos and Sam were sitting round the kitchen table, mugs of tea in their hands.

Mrs T ushered them in. "Tea?"

"Mimi will have one," Jannie replied, "I'd like a word with Sam outside, if I may?"

Sam jumped up. "Can I bring Aggie?"

"Ja, come on."

They walked across the fields towards the cove, Aggie racing ahead of them as Sam told Jannie how he was training her. "Look," he said, giving a sharp whistle. The puppy stopped and sat down, looking at Sam. She raced off when Sam whistled again. "That is her first lesson," he told Jannie earnestly. "Next I will teach her to come."

"That is very impressive, jonge." Jannie smiled at the boy. They continued down to the cove, Sam chattering excitedly about training Aggie, and his work on the farm.

"Let's sit here." Jannie pointed to a wave-smoothed rock on the high tide line.

Sam called Aggie and lifted her onto his knee; Jannie sat beside him and lit a cigarette. Inhaling deeply before blowing a plume of smoke down wind, Jannie whispered, "Are you still getting those bad dreams?" Not pausing for an answer, he looked at the startled boy and told him, "I am."

"Oh Jannie," Sam's eyes filled with tears. He leant his head against the old man's shoulder.

Jannie shifted slightly and put his arm around Sam. Holding him tightly, Jannie continued, "I have nothing to do. No work, nothing. I never go to bed really tired, even after a long walk." He sighed. "I have only had one since we got married, but others are waiting." He looked at Sam, "Lurking in the shadows like devils." He took another deep breath. "One night I nearly throttled Mimi." Sam gasped. "She heard me having a nightmare and thought I was in pain. I grabbed her by the throat when she tried to wake me…" Jannie's faint voice trailed off. He reached over to fondle Aggie's silky ears before letting go of Sam and getting to his feet.

Sam watched as Jannie crunched slowly across the small round pebbles towards the water's edge. When Aggie started whining, Sam put her down; she ran after the old engineer and danced around his feet. He knew Jannie had more to tell him and feared what he would say.

Waiting for Sam to join him, Jannie riffled through the stones until he found three flat ones. Bending slightly, he sent one after the other skipping across the calm sea. Aggie barked but did not chase after them. Sam ran down and grabbed Jannie's arm. "Teach me, teach me."

Once Sam had got the knack, Jannie turned to him abruptly. "Listen jonge, Mimi and I have to go back to London." His voice was strained, almost harsh. "She has to work, and I must help her." He hurried on, sensing Sam's protest. "There is work to be done. Hard work, every day." He stopped as abruptly as he had started, put his hand gently under Sam's chin and lifted it until Sam met his eyes. "We have no choice." He looked deep into Sam's eyes. "You know that. It is the War."

"Fuck the war!" Sam burst out. "I hate this fucking war!"

"So do I, Sam." Jannie's voice was gentle. "We all do. But we have work to do. You on the farm. Miriam and I in London."

"I will come with you," Sam cried out.

"Nee, Sam." Jannie kept his voice soft and calm. "We promised your parents to keep you safe. Here is safe. London is not."

When Sam spat out another oath, Jannie held up his hand to silence him. "Listen Sam. When I feel bad about something, I'll pick up a lump of coal or a stone and spit my bad thoughts onto it, then chuck it onto the fire, or in the sea."

He picked up a round stone, spat on it and threw it far out to sea.

Sam did the same. Then he put his arms around Jannie, his head on his chest and whispered, "I love you, Jannie."

Chapter 13.

"I don't want to do that again."

Tears poured down Mimi's cheeks as Jannie closed the carriage door. He gave her his handkerchief. "Nee, Mimi, nor do I."

It was a long, slow and largely silent journey back to London. Exhausted by the emotion of their parting, Jannie and Miriam slept most of the way on that hot July day.

Not knowing what she might find when they arrived, Miriam was relieved to find her home clean, tidy and very much as it had been when they left. "Bless you, Mrs Coward," Miriam murmured as she walked into her kitchen and saw a vase of freshly cut roses on the table.

Ever practical, Jannie checked the cupboards and larder door before filling the kettle. "Indeed," he replied, "no need to go shopping this evening." He put his arm around Mimi's shoulders and moved her gently to her seat before opening the back door.

"Mijn God!" brought Mimi swiftly to his side. They gazed in horror at the Anderson Shelter, half-buried between the house and the 'hidden synagogue', built at the back of the little garden at the turn of the century, when thousands of Jews successfully fled persecution in Eastern Europe.

"I'm glad they left the roses," Mimi said as they went over to inspect the shelter.

"Ja, and there's enough earth on top to grow more." Jannie walked carefully down the earth steps, opened the metal door and peered inside. "Look at this." He held Miriam's hand as she joined him. "Bunks, a floor, even some bedding." He looked at her. "Someone has been busy,"

"And thoughtful." Mimi squeezed his hand. "I suppose we must be thankful, but…"

"But nothing, my love." Jannie smiled at her. "Whoever did this saved me a job." He closed the door and tugged her back to the small patch of grass that was left. "I was dreading having to do that."

"At least we can still get here easily enough," Mimi said as she walked past it to open the door to the synagogue. "We'll have to get some help to change this around."

Jannie looked at the big room with fresh eyes as he considered how to turn it from a study into a place where people could sit, eat a simple meal, meet friends and rest in reasonable comfort. They had talked of little else in Cornwall.

"Come my dear, it's been a long day and we can sort this out in the morning."

She knew Jannie was thinking about Sam, how they could have worked together and how much he was missing him. So was she. The thought brought sudden tears to her eyes. Wiping them away surreptitiously, she said brightly, "Let's see what Mrs Coward has left us for supper."

They did not close the shutters or black-out curtains in the sitting room, preferring to leave the windows open. Carefully shielding the match with his hands, Jannie lit two cigarettes before joining Mimi on the sofa. She lay her head on his shoulder with a sigh. "Here we are, Mr Jansen, home at last."

Jannie kissed her ear and whispered, "It is very strange to be here, mevrouw." Pulling her closer, he added, "As your husband."

Twisting round to look at him, Mimi asked, "Why so, my dear?"

Jannie shrugged. "It is…"His brow furrowed as he sought the right words. "It was your home with Ike… I am a stranger holding his wife. Do you understand?"

"Oh Jannie," Mimi stopped him talking with a kiss. "Of course I understand. But now I am your wife. You must not worry about the past." She gazed intently at him. "We have each other. That is enough."

A little later Jannie whispered, "You are very persuasive, my dearest love."

And that was all they ever said about the matter.

Chapter 14.

Jannie and Mimi took the bus to the Dutch Embassy to register their marriage, travelling in the front seat on the top deck. "Just like children," chuckled Miriam.

London had changed little in the weeks they had been away, though the people seemed to be going about their lives more purposefully. "Perhaps we think that because we have been on holiday," Mimi hazarded.

"I don't think so." Jannie had been looking at people's faces and seeing how serious many of them looked. "They look as if they are waiting for Hitler to invade."

"Or perhaps the bombers." They were both right, as they learnt later when talking to Mr Wilkins, their local air-raid warden.

The staff at the embassy brought out a bottle of Jenever, with their congratulations. Toasts were drunk to the newly married couple and to the defeat of Germany, then Jannie and Miriam left to stroll hand-in-hand down to the river.

"We came here before," Jannie told Mimi as they leant against the parapet, smoking and watching the river traffic. He turned to face her. "Henri knew we would be lovers." He smiled wistfully. "He told me not to be shy."

"I am glad you took his advice." Mimi took his hand and lifted it to her lips before straightening up. "Cup of tea and then home." She sighed. "Time to get busy, my dear. We'll register with the Town Hall and police station, then find Mr Wilkins. He'll know what's needed and who can help us. I'll ring Harold after lunch."

"It's the old folks I'm worried about, Mrs Cohen." Mr Wilkins was standing in the middle of the synagogue. "There's lots of them alone now, what with mothers and children being evacuated, and men joining up."

He coughed. "Sorry. I mean, Mrs Jansen. If you could do something for them, that would be ever so good." He looked at her. "But they don't want no charity. You know that, don't you?"

Miriam knew that very well. She and Ike had learnt the hard way how proud and fiercely independent her East End neighbours were, especially those who had almost nothing of their own.

"We are thinking of having a social club in here," she explained. "Open to all. Somewhere to meet, get a cup of tea, maybe a bowl of soup, read a newspaper, bring their knitting or mending." She smiled at him. "They could pay a penny a week, or help to run the place."

Mr Wilkins looked pleased. "That should work." He looked around the room. "You'll have to make a few changes here."

Miriam nodded. "More than a few. We'll need help moving Ike's desk and chair." She thought for a minute. "Also his armchair, a few of his books and the rugs. Everything else can be given away, unless it's useful.."

"And finding chairs and tables," added Jannie. "Also, big pans, kettles, crockery and cutlery."

"That won't be difficult." Mr Wilkins beamed. "I know the janitor of the Free School. He'll have everything you need now it's been closed." He turned to Jannie. "They was evacuated last year 'cos of the bombing." Looking embarrassed, he said, "You, er, might need to slip him a bob or two."

"Bob?" enquired Jannie.

"Yus," Mr Wilkins rubbed his thumb over his fingers. "You know. Help him make his mind up." He smiled guilelessly. "It's an old habit round here. Makes the wheels go round."

"Ah," Jannie smiled back, "Bakshish. I understand." They shook hands solemnly.

Closing the door behind Mr Wilkins, Miriam turned to Jannie. "The East End lives by its own code of honour, my love, as you have just been told." She put her arms around him and laid her head against his shoulder. "It's how it has always been. Ike and I found it very difficult to begin with." She sighed. "But we learnt quickly, adapted and, in the end, saw very little wrong with it."

Jannie smiled. "It's much the same in ports the world over." He kissed the top of her head. "You never steal from your friends, never from the poor and seldom for yourself." He chuckled. "How much will we have to give Mr Wilkins?"

Mimi laughed. "Am I married to a pirate?"

"Nee, my dear, those really are bad people." Jannie shook his head. "Not a pirate. The English Navy calls it rabbiting." He held out a hand to his wife as he asked, "Will you show me Ike's workshop?"

Miriam looked at her suddenly serious man. She knew he understood this would be painful for her; it had been untouched since Ike died. She kissed him lightly, unlocked the door to the cellar and turned the light on. "Go on. I'll come in a minute."

Mrs Coward had obviously been down recently for there were no cobwebs, the floor had been swept and the work-bench and vice dusted. Apart from several saws hanging from wooden pegs on one wall, Ike's tools were in chests beneath the bench fitted to the far end. Various lengths of timber were neatly stacked on brackets on the back wall while the basement window was hidden behind thick wooden shutters, held closed by two lengths of iron sitting in iron brackets. Jannie turned to Miriam when she came down, a wide smile on his face, "Paradise, my dear." He took her in his arms and murmured "Thank you," as he hugged her.

Laughing, Miriam freed herself. "I'll call you when lunch is ready. You'll find some aprons hanging behind the door."

Sitting together on the kitchen step after lunch while they drank the last of the coffee Jannie had brought with him from Holland; "It's tea from now on, my love." Miriam leant her head against Jannie's shoulder. "I never expected this." She kissed him. "Never in a hundred years." Sighing contentedly, she closed her eyes and asked, "Am I your 'kindly widow'?"

"Ja, mijn liefste, since the day we met." He put his arm around her and whispered "You are my own true love; you have my heart as I have yours. By just exchange one to the other given."

Mimi finished Sir Philip Sydney's poem, "My true love hath my heart and I have his. There never was a better bargain given."

London was quiet that sunny afternoon, and they were content.

Chapter 15.

Miriam took one last lingering look at the room Ike had made his own before the removal men arrived to take away what remained of his furniture. She had given his elegant knee-hole desk and chair to Jannie, as well as the old leather armchair in which he used to sit and read. These went into Sam's old room once his bed had been moved up to the lacemakers' room. The beautiful Persian rugs were rolled up and put under the spare beds.

Neither she nor Jannie thought anything would survive the bombing, but neither said a word as they and Mrs C swept, dusted and wiped the room. The old synagogue looked enormous with only empty bookshelves lining the back wall.

"Well, Mrs C, what do you think we should get from the school?" Jannie had his own ideas but recognised that Mrs Coward would know what was wanted now she had agreed to help them run the centre.

Ever practical, she replied, "Two of them folding dinner tables and four benches. Four round tables, sixteen upright chairs and any couches and armchairs we can fit in." She scratched her head as she pictured what else they might need. "We'll need a table for the kitchen, an electric boiler, big saucepans, kettles, frying pans and all the crockery and cutlery we can get hold of. A dresser or cupboard. And tea pots, the bigger the better."

"No glasses," cut in Jannie. "Tin mugs will be safer."

"We had better let Mr Wilkins have a list for the janitor. What's his name, Nellie?" Miriam was amazed at how well organised Mrs C was and knew she would be leaning heavily upon her experience and wisdom.

"That is Mr Edelman," she smiled at Mimi. "He's alright, though the kids was scared of him." She laughed. "Until they got to know him."

"What about a cooker? We haven't talked about that," Jannie looked at the women.

"We'll pick one up at the school," Mimi replied, "an electric oven with six rings on top and a hot plate."

"We're not feeding the five thousand," chimed in Nellie. "No more than twenty at a time." She looked at Mimi. "We'd better pick up a blackboard, easel and a box of chalk." Seeing Jannie looking puzzled, she explained, "To write the menu on."

"Paper and pencils too," Jannie added, "and crayons. And anything else we see that'll come in handy."

"I told you he was a pirate," Mimi said to Nellie as they stubbed out their cigarettes and fetched their bags. "We'll have to keep him under control."

Jannie shrugged and followed them out.

Mr Edelman was as good as gold and would not take a penny from Mimi. "It's not for you. It's for the old folks," he explained. "And the kids."

Everything they had asked for was neatly packed up, boxes were labelled, furniture stacked near the gates to the school playground. A gleaming cooker stood to one side. "You'll find everything you need, Mrs Cohen. And if it's not here, let me know and I'll bring it round."

Leading them into the school, he said, "Alf will be here in a minute. There's just time for a cuppa." Alf was his mate; he had a lorry and friends who would help, and Mrs Edelman wanted to know all about Mrs Jansen's plans.

By the time the lorry was unloaded, the synagogue had been transformed into a creditable social club. Mrs Edelman now knew all about Mimi's plans and was busy recruiting her friends to help. Not for nothing had she been the head dinner lady for fifteen years, not that she would dream of telling Mrs Jansen how to run the kitchen.

"Come in, Mr Wilkins, and tell us what you think." Miriam ushered the indefatigable Air Raid Warden through the house and into the synagogue.

"Very good, Mrs Jansen, if I may say so." He walked around, impressed by the thought that had gone into the preparation before peering into the small room by the door. "Is this your only toilet?"

"Ja meneer," Jannie replied. "We also have buckets, disinfectant and I will put curtains up tomorrow."

Wilkins nodded. "I should brick them windows up if I was you. You don't want no glass flying about in here." When Jannie nodded, he carried on, "Can't do nothing about the house but you'd better reinforce the basement. I'll get some lumber for you."

With that he left.

"Oh Jannie," Miriam whispered, her face pale, "What are we doing?" She moved slowly towards him, her hands shaking as she ran her fingers over the backs of the chairs. He led her out into the evening sun and wrapped his arms around her.

"What we planned, my dear. Providing a haven for the lost and lonely." He massaged her shoulders, trying to relax her.

"But what about the bombs?" Miriam was close to tears, her stomach knotted and aching.

"We have our shelter." Jannie walked her slowly towards the house. "And no-one will be in the synagogue." He stopped and turned to face her. "I will make another shelter in the basement for anyone who needs it." He drew her close. "I will keep you safe, my dearest girl." He kissed her forehead. "I promise you."

Jannie closed his eyes, not wanting her to see the fear in them.

Chapter 16.

After a week of hot, hard work in the synagogue and basement, Jannie and Miriam walked through Wapping for an early evening drink in The Town of Ramsgate, a riverside pub Henri and he had discovered.

Mimi found a table overlooking the river while Jannie bought their drinks. She felt awkward, conscious of being the only woman present apart from the landlady. Turning her back on the room, she was immediately lost in the beauty of the evening light as it sparkled and fractured in the wake of a passing tug and tow.

"That's *Katie B*, going down with four." The strange voice behind her made Mimi jump.

"Sorry, ma'am, I didn't mean to frighten you." Miriam turned, looked up and saw a flustered, weather-beaten man of about fifty. "Your husband told me to come over."

She smiled at the look of relief on his face when Jannie pushed through the crowded room with two pints and a glass of beer.

"My love, this is Captain Abel."

Mimi was soon drawn into the world of a working London tug captain as Jannie plied him with questions. Tom Abel needed little encouragement to entertain them with stories of life on the river. Mimi found they had much in common, having lived in the East End for the past twenty years. Jannie sat back, entranced at the sight of his beautiful wife and this warm-hearted seaman chatting away like old friends. He was brought back into the conversation when Tom said, "Miriam tells me you're a ship's engineer. You kept that very quiet."

Jannie sighed. "I was until a few weeks ago." He looked at Mimi. "Now I am happily working with my wife."

"Hmm." Tom looked from one to the other. "I can see that." He passed his cigarettes around, lit them and continued. "Have you considered going back to sea?"

"Nee, Tom, nor will I."

"What about working on the river?"

"I did that for twenty years."

Tom looked surprised, but Jannie did not offer any explanation.

"Why are you asking?" Mimi was curious.

"We're already short of good men," Tom replied quietly. "More and more rivermen and dock workers are being conscripted into the Services. It'll get worse as time goes on. There'll be a shortage of engineers and …"

"And you think Jannie is a good engineer." Miriam raised an eyebrow. "Why is that"

Tom smiled at her. "Intuition. I've been around engineers all my working life. Your husband doesn't say much, and doesn't have to. He has an air of quiet competence about him." He paused to look at Jannie. "And his hands are an engineer's hands."

Miriam laughed. "You mean, still filthy."

Tom laughed as he stood. "Let me get you another drink."

When he had gone Jannie put his hands on Miriam's. "They aren't that filthy." He lifted them up and looked at them. "Maybe another month and they'll be clean."

"Is that what you want, my dear – clean hands?"

"I know what Tom wants." His eyes clouded. "I finished with ships when I left *De Ruyter*." Choking on his words, "After we buried Henri and Dirk."

Jannie looked at Miriam for a long moment. "You are all I have, Mimi. I will never leave you."

"So be it." Miriam held his hand to her cheek.

A slight breeze from the river cut through the cloud of cigarette and pipe smoke as Tom returned. Miriam had not been down to Wapping for several years and a strange pylon in Surrey Docks caught her eye. "What on earth is that?" she asked Tom.

"Ah." Tom drew his chair a little closer and leant forward. "That," he said quietly, "is a look-out tower. They've put them up in all the docks." Before Miriam could ask, he leant even closer. "Manned in air-raids to plot where gas bombs are dropped."

Miriam blanched. Ike had told her about gas attacks in the trenches and she knew men whose lungs had been ruined by it. She had seen the yellow pillar boxes but discounted the stories of gas attacks as alarmist.

Instinctively she put her hand on her gas-mask case. "I never thought we would need these."

Jannie touched her arm. "They didn't use gas in Holland. They didn't have to. Fire bombs and high explosives were enough."

Miriam looked from him to Tom. "They must be brave to do that. Are they soldiers?"

"Lord no," laughed Tom, "stevedores and labourers. Looking after their docks and their families."

"In that order," breathed Miriam to herself before replying brightly, "doing their duty."

Chapter 17.

A sudden, prolonged, unearthly scream was followed by a muffled *whoomph* that rattled the windows. Jannie leapt out of bed and froze, his breathing ragged, eyes wide, stomach knotted. Miriam flung back the bedclothes and went to him, reaching for his trembling hands.

It was 0015 on Sunday 25th August 1940. The first bomb, a large incendiary device, had just been dropped on the City of London.

The earlier air raid warning had turned out to be a false alarm. They ignored the second one and stayed in bed, having just spent an uncomfortable hour in the shelter.

Miriam picked up her torch and turned it on before leading Jannie slowly, silently, down the stairs to the kitchen. Having checked the blackout curtains she switched the electric light on and was relieved that nothing seemed to be broken, though flat surfaces were covered in a fine dust. She brushed a chair clean with her hand. "Sit here, Jannie." She shook him lightly until his eyes focussed on her. "Stay here, my love. I'll just look outside."

People were milling about aimlessly. She heard repeated questions; "Anyone hurt? Where did it land? What's happening?" and no answers.

Eventually Mr Wilkins appeared, red-faced and sweating beneath his white ARP helmet, pushing his way through the crowd and repeating, "It was a bomb on Fore Street. The All Clear has gone."

Miriam shut out the hubbub and leant against the door, breathing hard. That was too close for comfort and Jannie's reaction scared her. Instinctively she realised he could not stay here, not once the Germans started bombing in earnest. She also knew she needed help.

Jannie had boiled the kettle while Mimi was outside. "Sorry, my dear, it's engineer's tea." He smiled faintly. "Old habits die hard."

He held out his still trembling hands as he whispered, "But I can't pour it."

"Sit down, my love. I'll do that." She added a generous measure of brandy to each mug and sat beside him, lighting two cigarettes as she did.

They did not talk as they sipped tea and smoked; the silence frequently broken by Jannie's mug rattling against his teeth. Stubbing out her cigarette, Miriam got up and stood behind him. Placing her hands on his shoulders, she began to knead the tension out of his muscles, much as she had done for Ike when he came home from the Western Front.

Eventually Jannie's hands stopped trembling. He leant back and looked up at her. "I don't know what's wrong with me. I've never felt like this before."

Kneeling at his side, Miriam put a hand to his neck and gazed tenderly at her troubled husband. "You are worn out, my dear, stretched too thin." She stroked his cheek. "That bomb …"

"That bomb!" Jannie interrupted. "I thought we were being attacked." His face was drawn, his body tense. "Just like that first morning in Rotterdam."

"Tell me what happened," Miriam whispered, remembering how she had been able to draw some of the pain out of Ike by getting him to talk. She pulled him to his feet. "In the sitting room."

Chapter 18.

"We knew the Germans would come." Even though Jannie was leaning against Miriam, her arm around him, she struggled to hear what he was saying. "But the speed and violence were shocking." He twisted on the sofa to look at her. "Hundreds of aircraft flying over the city, the noise fading. The sky full of pigeons and sparrows, thousands of them. Then they came back, lower, louder, faster." Jannie locked his fingers together. "Then the bombing started. Attacking the airfield at Waalhaven. Dive bombers screaming down. Others circling, dropping fire bombs and high explosives. It was hell unleashed."

Miriam listened, appalled, as Jannie described how they had watched the attack, seaplanes landing on the river almost beside them, buildings burning, the desperate battle for the bridges. His eyes were closed and his voice hoarse. Putting her fingers lightly against his lips, she whispered, "Enough, my love. That's enough." She eased herself from his side, stood and poured them two small whiskies.

She topped them up with water before handing one to Jannie as she sat beside him. "What time was this?"

"Early, it was just getting light." Jannie sighed. "It went on all day, and all we could do was pray they didn't hit us." He looked at Miriam. "Can you imagine what that was like?" She shook her head. "We had to keep busy. Especially Sam. He was worried sick about his parents. Blaming himself they hadn't got away. God, it was dreadful." Jannie's eyes filled with tears. He shook his head and exhaled noisily.

Miriam sat very still as Jannie struggled to regain control. Once his breathing slowed, he opened his eyes and reached for her. "Oh my love, we were so helpless."

She drew his head to her shoulder, stroking his cheek as she whispered, "Yet you escaped. Right under the nose of those bastards."

Jannie gave a great gust of laughter at Mimi's sudden, unexpected profanity. He shook his head in wonder, gazing at this remarkable woman who was now his wife.

"Well, you did, didn't you?" Inwardly rejoicing, Miriam struggled to keep from laughing with him. "And not just you but all the others too."

"Yes my love, we did." Scowling, he added, "But not Sam's family."

"Was there anything you could have done about that?" Miriam knew the answer but needed Jannie to say it.

"Nee, dammit. Nothing at all."

"And are they safe with Oom Paul?"

"As safe as anywhere in Holland."

Jannie stood, stretched and lit two cigarettes. Passing one to Miriam, he walked around the sitting room, picked up an ashtray and settled back on the sofa. He smiled at her.

"Thank you, my dearest girl."

Miriam kissed him. It was a start. She knew there was a long way to go.

Chapter 19.

"Lady Teagle, please."

Miriam was lucky the telephone was not engaged. Kent was bearing the brunt of continuous air attacks as Germany attempted to destroy the Royal Air Force and disrupt shipping in the Thames Estuary. Lines to the C-in-C's headquarters were always busy.

"Emma Teagle here. Who is that?"

Undaunted by the cut-crystal accent, Miriam replied, "Mrs Jansen. Jannie's wife. You wrote to us."

"Miriam? Is that you?"

"Yes, and I'm sorry to…"

"Don't be," cut in Emma. "What can I do for you? I don't mean to be rude, but these lines are terribly busy. Is it Sam?"

"Not Sam. Jannie. I need to get him out of London. They dropped a bomb near us and …"

"I understand," again Emma cut in. "How soon do you want to leave?"

"As soon as possible."

"Right. I'll make a call and ring back. In the mean-time you'd better get packed."

She hung up. Miriam stood in her office staring at the telephone, bemused by Lady Teagle's response. It was only eight hours since the bomb had gone off and her life was, once again, in turmoil.

"You had better make a list," Jannie teased her when she told him.

"I had better speak to Mrs Edelman and make sure she's happy to run the place without us, then get Harold to set up an account for it."

When Miriam had first envisaged turning the synagogue into a community centre, she always imagined she would be running it, with help from Jannie and a few others, notably Mrs Coward. In fact, once she had invited Mrs Edelman to help, it rapidly became obvious that she was the ideal person to be in charge. Not only did she have an intimate knowledge of what was required, but also the contacts necessary to keep the kitchen well stocked, the canteen staffed, and bakers by the dozen. All this, as Jannie had said one evening, in addition to having a heart as big as her ample bosom.

As she thought, Mrs Edelman was unfazed by the news and readily agreed to run the community centre, and Mrs Coward was happy to look after the house. Harold Hartley came round to make arrangements for paying the bills, suggesting that he agree a budget with the two women once they had been up and running for a month.

He took Miriam and Jannie out for an early lunch at The Gun in Spitalfields. "It's not where I had planned to celebrate your marriage," he told them as they went upstairs to the small dining room, "but they do serve the best steak and kidney pudding in the City."

While Miriam and he talked through the soup course about how he would keep an eye on the community centre, Jannie remained silent, stirring his soup with his spoon, eyes blank and face slack.

Harold coughed to catch his attention. Jannie lifted his head and blinked a couple of times. "I'm sorry, meneer, I was miles away."

"I've been there, Jannie," Harold spoke quietly. "In that dark place." He gazed at the engineer. "I did not have a wife then and it was bad."

"I would be lost without Miriam." Jannie took her hand. "But she should not have to go through this again."

Harold leant forward, looking from one to the other. "You are right. Of course you are. But it is because she has been through this before that she is much better able to help you now."

He leant back. "These are battles we have to face, those of us who have seen and heard terrible things, and they are always better faced with someone at our side."

Jannie nodded slowly. "Ja. I was able to keep Sam busy…"

"And safe," Mimi interrupted.

"And safe," Jannie agreed, "and Mr Trevasso will keep him safe; and so busy he has no time to think." He paused. "I thought I would be fine once we were married. Miriam drove the dreams away. I was so happy."

He looked down. "Until…" He took a deep, shuddering breath. "Until that bomb undid me."

The long silence was broken by Harold. "Courage is finite, Jannie. We use it up without realising it. You were drawing on your courage from the first moments of the invasion. I only know a little about what you went through, but I am not surprised you were undone by that bomb. It would have undone me when I came back from the last war."

Jannie looked at Miriam. "Not much of a wedding present, is it?"

"Oh Jannie, don't say that." Miriam squeezed his hand. "We will come through this together."

The arrival of a steaming suet pudding demanded their full attention when it was sliced open and meat and gravy spooned onto their plates, together with mashed potatoes, carrots and broad beans.

They agreed it was the best steak and kidney pudding any of them had tasted and the perfect way to celebrate their wedding.

Lady Teagle telephoned that afternoon.

"I'll have to be quick, Miriam. Take the ten o'clock train to Andover tomorrow morning. You'll be met there and taken to Saffron House. It's where Henk is. A friend of ours owns it. Part of it's a naval convalescent hospital. I've arranged for Jannie to see a doctor there." She laughed, a delicious tinkling laugh, "After all, he's probably still in the Navy."

Emma paused, as if checking her list. "Oh yes. Charles has a cottage for you. He doesn't want any rent, but would appreciate a little help around the place."

"Who is Charles?" Miriam asked.

Emma could not believe what she was hearing. "Colonel Blackhurst. He's a good friend."

The operator interrupted. "Finish you call please, milady. We need the line."

"Of course. Let me know how you get on. Bye."

Chapter 20.

Tuesday 28th August 1940

Waiting outside the red-brick station, their scant luggage at their feet, Jannie suddenly asked, "I wonder why it's called Saffron House? Like those buns we had in Cornwall."

Miriam loved his curiosity. "Perhaps it grows here." She was a city girl and knew little about plants.

"Maybe, but more likely someone made a lot of money importing it." Jannie knew saffron used to be rare and valuable. "Perhaps he was a pirate." Which was close to the truth and quickly forgotten in the excitement of seeing Henk sitting beside the driver of the pony and trap entering the station forecourt.

Henk jumped down, lifted Jannie off his feet and swung him around, laughing as he shouted in Dutch, "God, man, married already. You didn't waste any time." He stopped and went bright red.

"Sorry mevrouw, I forgot you speak Dutch," he stuttered, looking anywhere but at the laughing Miriam.

"Oh Henk, it is good to see you again." She held out her arms to embrace him. "And when are *you* getting married?" It was a question Henk ignored.

They chatted merrily as the pony trotted along the road, driven, as they learnt, by Adam, one of the few men left to work the farm.

"Oh my word," breathed Miriam as they rounded a bend in the drive, "what a beautiful house."

An elegantly proportioned three-storey building, flanked by two wings, stood at the top of a field that rose gently from a river. Facing south against a background of mature trees, it looked to Miriam and Jannie like a palace.

As Adam brought the pony to a halt abreast the door to the west wing, it opened and an upright, white-haired gentleman walked over to help Miriam alight. "Welcome," he smiled, shaking hands with her and Jannie. "Come and meet my wife."

Henk followed them into the sitting room.

Lady Blackhurst was kneeling on the floor playing with a little girl who squeaked with delight and ran over to Henk. She tidied away the toys and stood to welcome the new arrivals.

Amid the handshakes and introductions Miriam studied her hosts with care, relaxing as she took in their easy manner and evident kindness. It was difficult for Jannie to relax. He believed he had failed his wife, that his reaction to the explosion had diminished him in her eyes. He was standing slightly apart from the others, looking down at his feet when a hand touched his face. Flinching, he jerked his head away before seeing the little girl in Henk's arms.

She looked at him solemnly, her brown eyes wide. "Are you Jannie?" she asked in Dutch.

Joy flooded through Jannie; this must be the little girl who had been put onboard *De Ruyter* by her mother and father. He remembered hearing how they could not go themselves. Something about their parents refusing to leave. Henk had told him he found her standing by the guard-rail and how she clung to him when he picked her up. And that was also when he got to know Sarah; they had never let her go – or each other.

"Ja, mijn lieve meisje. I am Jannie. Are you Ruth?"

When Ruth nodded, Jannie told her, "I am very pleased to meet you."

Lady Blackhurst came over to introduce herself. "She's been talking about you all morning. Hallo Jannie, I'm Liz. I am so glad you are here." She took his arm and steered him a few paces away from the others before saying quietly, "You have a most beautiful wife. I gather you've only been married a few weeks."

"I am very lucky, milady. She is beautiful. And you are very kind to invite two more strangers to stay with you."

"It is the least we can do." Liz looked at his troubled face, noting the slight tremor in his voice. "Emma told us you need to get away from London. We have an empty cottage." She laid a hand on his arm. "This is a good place to be," she laughed as she steered him to her husband, "and I think you might enjoy some of Charlie's gadgets."

"What has she been telling you?" Sir Charles was a gentle man, deeply concerned by the impact of another world war on those fighting to defeat the same enemy he had fought so recently.

"She was talking about your gadgets, milord." Charles's eyebrows rose at the use of his elevated status, but he said nothing. His knighthood meant little to him.

He laughed. "My gadgets. Huh! Well, we have a turbine to generate electricity, a motorised fire pump, and a tractor on order, though it will be some time before that arrives." He thought for a moment. "She probably means my workshop, and perhaps the forge." He looked at Jannie. "We can always use an extra pair of hands." Suddenly serious. "But only when you're ready."

Equally serious, Jannie replied. "I need to work, milord. I need to work so hard I have no time to think, so hard I sleep without dreams. That is what I need."

"I know, Jannie. I also know it might help to talk to one of the doctors here. They came when the Navy evacuated part of Haslar and took over the house and east wing." Seeing Jannie's puzzled expression, he explained, "The naval hospital near Portsmouth. It was partially evacuated at the beginning of the war. This is a convalescent hospital. *HMS Saffron* they call it, though we don't fly any flags or have a parade ground. Not even a sentry at the gate." He chuckled. "Don't want to draw attention to the place."

"It's also a working farm," said Liz as she rejoined them. "Mostly arable, as instructed by the Ministry, with a herd of Jerseys for milk, and also chickens, geese and pigs."

"And your horses," reminded Sir Charles.

"And my horses. Do either of you ride?" She looked disappointed when Jannie and Miriam shook their heads. "That's a pity. Ruth is learning, and so is Sarah." She smiled. "Henk refuses to."

"Ja, milady." Henk rejoined them as the door opened and the cook announced, "Lunch is on the table."

Sarah rushed in, pink and breathless. "I'm sorry I'm so late, milady, but it's nearly ready." She smiled with delight when she saw Jannie, holding out her hand to greet him. Jannie bowed as he shook it. "Meet my wife. Miriam, meet Sarah."

Lunch was a merry meal. Salad, cold meat, cold trout, cheese, butter and freshly baked bread. The Blackhursts were excellent hosts, their guests relaxed, and Ruth behaved beautifully in her high chair.

Learning that Jannie only had his uniform and a pair of dungarees, Lady Blackhurst took him upstairs to her son's bedroom. She took a tweed jacket and a pair of grey flannel trousers from the wardrobe and a couple of flannel shirts from a chest of drawers. "These should fit," she told him. "Leave your uniform here and I'll get it cleaned and pressed."

She stood in the middle of the room for a moment. "I nearly forgot." She got a pair of braces out of a drawer and a waistcoat from the wardrobe before leaving Jannie to get changed.

Chapter 21.

"We must be the luckiest people in the world." Miriam was gazing out of the sitting room window at the roses in the front garden of the cottage the Blackhursts had given them, her head on Jannie's shoulder and one arm around his waist.

She smiled at him. "And you, my dear, look very distinguished in those clothes."

Jannie laughed. "It is strange to be out of uniform." He looked at her. "Strange but good. I shall have to buy my own clothes to work in. I don't want to spoil these." He tucked his thumbs into his waistcoat pockets and rocked to and fro on his heels. "Also some shoes." Holding out his leg, he laughed again. "My boots don't look right, do they?"

They wandered slowly around the south facing sitting room, into the parlour at the back and the large kitchen before going upstairs. There was a big bedroom over the kitchen, a smaller one next to it, and a bathroom and separate lavatory, all spick and span after Sarah's busy morning; there were also fresh flowers in the sitting room, kitchen and their bedroom. "Lady Blackhurst picked those," Sarah explained when she showed them round.

Miriam took off her shoes and lay back on the bed, delighted it was so comfortable. Giving a contented sigh, she patted the cover beside her. "I think we will be very happy here."

Jannie sat in the small armchair, gazing at her. "I think so too. There is plenty of work for me. Henk said so. Machinery to service, repairs to be done, and help needed around the farm." He smiled slightly. "And Ruth told me I have to read her stories."

Miriam laughed. "The little minx. That's what she told me." She turned onto her side, propping herself on her elbow. "It's a miracle she's here. And that Sarah and Henk are so good with her."

"And with each other," Jannie added. "I'm glad they're our neighbours."

The two cottages were on the other side of a tennis court and walled garden, and had been empty since the beginning of the War. Originally built by the Blackhursts for their senior domestic staff, the cottages were fully furnished, warm, connected to mains electricity, with water pumped from a well to tanks in their roofs, and drains connected to a septic tank. The War had brought great changes to the estate. With its young staff called up, the few remaining elderly domestic staff now lived in quarters in the west wing of the big house.

"Come on." Jannie helped Miriam off the bed. "Let's go for a walk." They were both curious to explore their new surroundings. Lady Blackhurst had given them a sketch map of the estate and pointed out a few walks.

It was so hot that Jannie changed into his cotton dungarees and an old shirt. Mimi, wearing a yellow summer frock and her straw hat, took Jannie's arm. "Let's find the farm. Sam wants to know if they have any cows."

Sarah was taking in the washing as they walked past and called out, "Where are you going?"

"To find the farm."

"Can I come with you? Ruth needs a walk."

Mimi saw how pleased Jannie looked. "We'd love that."

They followed Sarah into her kitchen where they were greeted by an ecstatic young golden retriever. Mimi folded the washing while Sarah woke Ruth from her afternoon nap. Once the dog had calmed down, Jannie picked up a newspaper from the table, its headline shouting NAZIS RAID LONDON – AND 13 TOWNS.

He dropped it when he heard Ruth scampering down the stairs. She burst into the kitchen; and stopped. Eyes wide open, she put her thumb into her mouth and stared from one to the other. She had Henk's pocket watch in her free hand.

Sarah was a few paces behind, laughing as she knelt beside Ruth. "You remember Jannie, don't you?"

When Ruth nodded, she went on, "They are going for a walk. Shall we go with them?

Jannie and Miriam were amazed at the size of the Saffron estate and by how few people were working there. "All the young men have been called up," Sarah explained. "Old Adam looks after the horses. He's the ploughman, drives the trap when Liz doesn't, and the cart on market day.

Connie and Elsie, the Land Army girls, live here. Others come and help when we need more hands. Their houses are part of the farm buildings. About quarter of a mile from the east wing." She looked at Jannie, "That's where the Colonel has his workshop. There's a garage as well."

Seeing Ruth wilting in the heat, Jannie knelt down and asked, "Would you like a piggy back?"

Ruth looked from him to Sarah and back again before shyly nodding.

Those were the first of many miles that Jannie carried the little girl on his shoulders, her legs dangling on his chest, his hands clasping her ankles. As they set off, he asked, "Would you like me to tell you a story?"

Ruth leant forward to whisper in his right ear, "Yes please."

And so Jannie started; "Once upon a time there was a little boy called Jan. He lived with his mummy and daddy in a little house by a big river…"

Miriam glanced at them, saw Ruth entranced and the joy in Jannie's face. She turned away quickly lest he saw the tears in her eyes and dropped a few paces behind. Sarah took her arm without a word.

Miriam stopped, blinking away her tears. "I can't see." She fumbled for her handkerchief, wiped her eyes and blew her nose before saying, "Ike never had a chance to do that."

"Ike?" Sarah knew nothing of Miriam's life.

While Jannie was telling Ruth about his early childhood, Miriam told Sarah about her husband and babies, and how Ike was killed. Sarah in turn told her why her parents insisted she leave Holland and why they stayed to look after her father's patients. Brushing away her tears, she stopped, took both Miriam's hands in hers and hugged her, before whirling her round, laughing. "And now I have Ruth and you have Jannie."

Her joy was infectious. "And Henk?" Miriam smiled, "When are you marrying him?"

Sarah blushed a deep pink. "Are you a match-maker, Tante Mimi?"

"No, my dear, just a nosy old woman."

Jannie was waiting for them in the shade of an oak tree, watching as Ruth ran back to Sarah.

Both women laughed when he said "Let's find Henk." Looking puzzled he went on, "It's too hot to go much further."

The path took them through woods dappled with pools of light, across a small meadow full of flowers, to the river where Henk was putting his tools in a barrow.

As Ruth ran to him, Sarah stopped Jannie and Miriam. "Watch this." Henk dropped to all fours so Ruth could climb onto his back. At her cry of "Gee up!" Henk crawled as fast as he could along the river bank, down a slope and splashed into a shallow pool amid shrieks and bellows and fountains of spray.

"Go on!" Sarah could see that Jannie was itching to join them. With a quick grin, he took off his boots and socks and sat on the edge, savouring the cool water running over his feet.

Henk and Ruth splashed their way out of the river as Sarah and Miriam came to sit alongside Jannie. "We'd be soaked if we'd brought Sheba."

Abandoning Henk, Ruth came up behind Jannie and put her wet arms around his neck. "Carry me," she demanded, heedless of her soaking clothes.

"Only as far as the drive," he groaned, levering himself to his feet.

"Why?"

Never having had children of his own, Jannie was unaware of their restless curiosity and imperious ways.

"Why?" he said, hoisting her onto his shoulders. "Why do you think?" He stretched out a leg and wiggled his toes. It was the first of many 'whys', several of which were difficult to answer, especially as Ruth got older.

They set off, the others following. "I never knew Jannie liked children," Henk rumbled. "He's always struck me as a very private person," adding, when he saw Mimi's surprise, "he kept himself to himself."

"Well," said Miriam, "He is very shy; at least, he was when we first met." She sighed. "It was Henri who changed him."

"Henri?" Henk stopped in surprise, put the barrow down and asked, "What did Henri do?"

Miriam gave a little laugh. "He saw how Jannie looked at me, how he behaved. Henri must have been watching me too because he asked him if I was 'the kindly widow' he had been searching for." She laughed delightedly. "All in Dutch, in front of me, not knowing I understood every word. And just before Dunkirk he told him that now was not the time to be shy."

Miriam saw Sarah's expression as she looked at Henk and smiled to herself. "Come on, we'd better catch them. Jannie needs his boots."

None of them forgot that afternoon. It was the start of a close, lifelong friendship between five very different people.

Chapter 22.

The colonel saw Jannie pass his study window and went out to meet him. "Come on in, Jannie. The doctor's here." He recognised Alan's clothes and thought they suited the old Dutchman.

Jannie bowed slightly as he shook the colonel's hand. "Good morning, milord." Remaining standing and looking very formal, he continued, "We did not expect such kindness, nor such a comfortable home." He bowed again. "Thank you."

Turning to the young doctor, he shook his hand. "It is kind of you to be here, meneer. I am not sure what you can do for me. Perhaps listening to the colonel and I talk will give you some idea."

Sir Charles, deeply moved by Jannie's simple sincerity and impressed by the manner with which he sidelined the doctor, took a moment to gather his thoughts. "We are fortunate to live here, Jannie, and delighted to be able to help you and your wife. You have a good friend in Henk and he told us all about you and Mrs Jansen." He studied Jannie. "Lady Teagle told me what you did at Dunkirk…" He paused, "and what it cost …"

"The cost was high, milord, but the reward was great." Jannie shrugged. "What else could we do?"

"You could have let the Navy take your ship," the colonel replied as he ushered Jannie to a seat. "Make yourself comfortable while I see about some tea. We have a lot to talk about."

"Mind if I join you?" asked Lady Blackhurst, backing through the door with a plate of biscuits in her hand and not waiting for an answer.

Jannie shook his head and helped her to her seat. The colonel returned with four mugs of tea, put them on the table and sat down.

"Liz will tell you about the farm in a minute and then we'll have a look at my gadgets." He snorted. "One day she'll be glad of them." She smiled at him and passed the biscuits to Jannie.

Sitting up straight and looking Jannie in the eye, the colonel asked quietly, "Would you like to tell us what made you leave London?"

Jannie gave a soft "huh" accompanied by a crooked smile. "Miriam, milord." He looked at Lady B. "She knows me better than I know myself."

Sitting very still, he told them how their ship was at the heart of the battle for the bridges in Rotterdam when the Germans launched their surprise attack on neutral Holland on the 10th May; how they watched the relentless bombing, about Sam and why his family could not escape onboard *De Ruyter*, and how they found Tante Mimi.

His voice dropped to little more than a whisper when he told them about the three times they sailed to Dunkirk, and what it was like to be in the engine room with the hull ringing as bombs and shells exploded around them, how he had to keep Sam and Fred Firth so busy they had no time to think, about the time none of them moved when a series of explosions marched ever closer, the last one rocking the ship without damaging her.

He stopped abruptly, looked down, closed his eyes and, in a voice so soft they had to strain to hear him, he told them about the violent concussion of the bomb that exploded alongside, lifting and throwing the ship about, how he and his engine room crew were tossed around like rag dolls, the shriek of escaping steam, and the relief at finding themselves still alive ... until he heard the sound of rushing water.

The battle to keep the ship afloat depended on him. No-one else could take his place, no corners could be cut until the ship was safe. All the time his thoughts were of Henri, seriously wounded on the bridge, with the ship stopped in the water, and of the other men wounded and killed in the attack.

Jannie took a deep breath, opened his eyes and sat upright. Looking from one to the other, he said, "That is what happened. I thought it was happening again when the bomb went off in London."

The only sound in the room was the ticking of the clock on the mantlepiece.

Liz was the first to move, wiping away her tears. Sir Charles blew his nose. Jannie reached for his cigarettes, stopped, took a sip of cold tea and stood up. "Could we walk a little outside, please?" He looked down at Lady Blackhurst. "In your garden?"

"Of course we can." She led him through her kitchen and out of the back door, across their tennis court and into the walled garden. Sir Charles followed with the doctor, picking up a packet of cigarettes and some matches on the way. He had noticed Jannie reaching for his before remembering they did not like people to smoke inside.

Liz tucked her arm under Jannie's as she led him past rows of vegetables interspersed with patches of flowers. Neither spoke. Jannie was unaware of his surroundings until they reached the far wall. "So much fruit." He turned to Lady Blackhurst, his eyes once more alive. "You do all this yourself?"

"I have help, Jannie." Liz smiled. "It's too much for me."

"Perhaps Mimi and I could help sometimes?" Jannie looked at her.

"I should like that." As Liz steered Jannie to a bench in the shade of the apple trees where the branches grew along wires strung between posts, Sir Charles fetched a couple of deck chairs from the potting shed. Jannie lit one of the proffered cigarettes and took a deep drag before blowing the smoke away.

"Henri died in my arms." He continued as if there had been no interruption. "I thought I was alright. I buried him and Dirk, and took *De Ruyter* back to Chatham. I promised Henri I would keep Sam safe and I did." In a stronger voice he repeated, "I did keep Sam safe."

He closed his eyes, remembering Sam's tears when they left. On opening them, he saw a bed full of pink roses and murmured, in a voice full of wonder, "Then Miriam married me." He shifted to look at Lady Blackhurst. "I promised to keep her safe." Moving as if uncomfortable and now looking at his feet, he whispered, "But I cannot." He took a deep, shuddering breath. "I cannot keep her safe."

Desperate, his voice hoarse, he said, "She drove away the nightmares. But one bomb falls, not near, and I am so frightened I cannot move."

Jannie shook his head as if to clear it. "Miriam had a husband who fought in the first War. She saw what it did to him and she was able to help him. He was killed by your police four years ago."

Shaken, Sir Charles asked, "What happened?"

Jannie told him. "I think she called it the battle of Cable Street. It was when English fascists wanted to march on the Jewish quarter; Irish dockers and Jews stopped them. The police were sent to clear a way for the fascists. Her husband was there." His voice was very quiet. "A child fell in the road. Meneer Cohen was trying to pick him up when a policeman on a horse hit him on his head with his truncheon. He died four days later without waking up." He looked at Sir Charles. "I do not understand how this could have happened here. Still, Miriam is not bitter. She says it was just one of those things."

Giving a quiet "huh" Jannie went on, "I cannot keep my wife safe so she brings me here, to save me."

There was a long, thoughtful silence before Liz stood. Taking Jannie by the hand, she said quietly, "That should not have happened. I am very sorry." When Jannie nodded, she continued. "Miriam brought you to a place where you can save yourself, didn't she Charles?"

Getting to his feet, Sir Charles put his hand under Jannie's other elbow and helped him stand. "It will take time, Jannie. Liz is right; this is a place where people find peace of mind. Sometimes in this garden, or in the woods, by the river, or…"

Jannie interrupted, "Or perhaps among your gadgets?" His eyes had cleared and he was smiling.

Looking from one to the other, he said, "It was hard to tell you these things. I did not want to speak of them. I think it is you, not this place, that helps people find peace of mind."

The doctor left without saying a word.

Chapter 23.

"I'll go and find Miriam," Liz called after Charles and Jannie as they headed over to the workshop.

Drawn to the sound of Ruth's laughter, she was not surprised to see Miriam and Sarah playing with the little girl under the trees at the back of the cottages. Ruth ran up to Liz, took her hand and towed her towards the open gate declaring, "I'm thirsty." Sarah and Mimi hurried over and they were soon settled round the kitchen table with a glass of home-made lemonade for Ruth, and the kettle boiling on the stove.

"Made with lemons from our greenhouse," Liz told Mimi.

Ruth was soon asleep in an armchair, with Sheba lying on the floor at her feet. Sarah poured tea for her guests and said to Mimi, "This is not what you had planned."

"No." She looked at her hands, looked up, and smiled. "It was not at all what we had planned. But," and here she sighed loudly. "what we *had* planned has come to pass. There is a social club in the old synagogue at the bottom of our garden and it doesn't need us to run it."

Her description of the work she and Ike did, and what she and Jannie had set up, fascinated Liz and Sarah, and many questions followed about her life in the East End. "You must write a book," Liz told her.

"Maybe, one day." Mimi smiled. "But first you must tell me how I can help here."

Glancing at Sarah, Liz replied, "There are several ways. The Navy may welcome help – reading to sailors, assisting them with letters, perhaps pushing wheelchairs." She hesitated. "But they have not asked for anything."

"There is something we have talked about," Sarah added. "There are a number of children in the village about the same age as Ruth and there's no room in the school for them."

"Most are evacuees," amplified Liz. "All sorts and sizes." She frowned. "Some with their mothers, but not many."

Miriam was puzzled. "But they were evacuated last September. What have they been doing since then?"

"Ah, but when nothing happened, they went home. It's only since Dunkirk that some have started coming back." Liz looked at Miriam, "Many more will come when the Germans start bombing in earnest."

"And no room in the school?"

"But plenty of room here," said Sarah, "and one little girl who needs company; and an education."

"What sort of education?" Mimi was intrigued.

"The basics," Sarah replied without hesitation. "Being kind and honest, living peacefully with others, telling the truth, sharing." She looked at Liz and Mimi. "Does that make sense?"

"I would encourage their curiosity." Liz thought for a moment. "Climbing the next hill to see what's beyond, and looking at what's beneath their noses." She laughed. "Metaphorically speaking."

"How old are these children?" Miriam had not been expecting those answers.

"Mainly three to five. Hopefully without too many bad habits." Liz laughed. "And not too many feral ones."

"Uh-huh." Mimi was puzzled. "Who will teach them, and how?"

Sarah replied. "We will. Through play, music, stories, going on walks, showing and making." She laughed, "Little steps for little people."

"I understand that, but why the emphasis on virtues?"

"Because I've heard too many stories of Nazis twisting the minds of children, Mimi, even turning them into spies who betray their own parents." Sarah spoke quietly but with great passion.

"We'll start with half a dozen, all three or four years old." Liz added. "Get them used to each other, and us. Build on small successes."

"We have much to do before we're ready." Sarah took over. "Preparing the room, creating the lessons, acquiring the tools we'll need: toys, books, materials."

"We have a wonderful playground all around us," Liz said. "Woods, fields, animals and…"

"The river," Sarah finished for her. "Henk is itching to teach them about it." She laughed. "He'd love to teach them to fish but Sir Charles isn't too keen."

"I think Jannie would like to help," mused Miriam, thinking of his sketches and his easy way with Ruth, her acceptance of him.

"And you?" asked Liz.

Miriam was dreading that question. Seeing Jannie carrying Ruth on his shoulders had awakened her agony; long-buried memories of her babies now flooded her mind. She shook her head. "I don't know," she sighed. "I just don't know."

Sarah took her hand. "Tell us, my dear, do you think our ideas are silly? That we should be teaching reading, writing and arithmetic?"

"Oh no. Not at all silly." Miriam was emphatic. "I'm not sure how you'll manage to teach those qualities, but the children will pick up the basics without even noticing. Getting them to make a cake would teach weights and measures, arithmetic too." She stopped, embarrassed lest she was talking nonsense.

"We hadn't thought of that." Miriam relaxed; Liz was obviously sincere. "We need more ideas like that. Perhaps you could have a think and jot some down."

"Time for a cuppa before we wake Ruth." Sarah led the way into the kitchen. She took an exercise book from a drawer and gave it to Miriam. "For ideas."

Chapter 24.

After a quick tour of the farm, the colonel led Jannie to an adjacent barn, unlocked the double doors and swung them open.

Pointing to a gleaming trailer he said, "My fire pump." Watching as Jannie moved around the pump, looking closely at the engine, controls and fire-fighting equipment, he explained, "She's a Coventry Climax. Pumps about 140 gallons a minute. The Navy's got a bigger one, pumps 500 gallons a minute."

Jannie was impressed. "How do you move yours?"

"My car." Sir Charles looked at Jannie. "With a crew of up to four people."

"Where do you get water? Surely the river's too far from the house and farm?"

The colonel was unsurprised by Jannie's quick grasp of the major problem. "You saw the pond in front of the house?" When Jannie nodded, he went on. "That's the closest and most reliable source. We've been topping it up recently from the river."

"Anywhere else?"

"There's a well in the farmyard, one behind the house and another between your cottages. They never run dry." The colonel crossed his fingers and moved over to his workbench. Jannie realised that, much as onboard *De Ruyter*, the farm was equipped to deal with most of the technical problems likely to be encountered. "Who works here?" he asked, and smiled when Sir Charles replied, "I do."

He led Jannie to a smaller, open-sided barn nestling against his workshop. "We also have a smithy."

"And a blacksmith?" The fire was cold and the place looked neglected.

"And a blacksmith," Sir Charles told him. "He comes up when a horse needs shoeing." Seeing Jannie's expression, he said, "Will Durrant. He's old and comes when we need him. His son worked here but got called up."

"Perhaps Mr Durrant could teach me." Jannie smiled. "I should like that."

"So would he. I'll ask him." The colonel was pleased by Jannie's interest in so many aspects of farm life. "We'll have a look at the pond now. I have a few ideas."

Jannie thought it was more of a lake than a pond. It lay at the west end of the field of wheat stubble in front of Saffron House. "This was a beautiful ornamental garden until September." The colonel looked sadly around him. "The Ministry insisted we grub out the trees and shrubs, plough it up and plant wheat." He cheered up when he told Jannie, "I persuaded them to leave the pond and the fountain." He laughed at the memory. "Told them it was the only source of water if the house caught fire." Grinning wickedly, he added, "And the fountain's the only way to keep it topped up."

"How does that work?"

"There's an electric pump which draws water from the river. It's powered by our water-turbine, same as the saw-mill. We'll look at those another day."

As they walked back to the house, Jannie said, "That doctor." He saw the colonel's eyes flicker. "He's not a real doctor, is he?" Not giving him time to reply, he went on, "And this is not a real hospital."

The colonel grimaced. "How did you know?"

"Age. Intuition." Jannie shrugged. "I don't think a real doctor could have sat there without saying anything."

"And," he went on, "it doesn't smell like a hospital."

"Come with me, Jannie." The colonel took Jannie's arm and led him back to the west wing. "You are right." He glanced at the house. "It is not a hospital and he is not a doctor. I would be grateful if you could keep this to yourself. It suits me and it suits the Navy for people to go on believing that."

"Of course, milord." Jannie stopped again. "You do not need to tell me anything else." He smiled at his worried host. "Perhaps you could tell them to sprinkle a little disinfectant around from time to time."

Chapter 25.

"Harvest time soon." Henk and Jannie were sitting in the garden, tea in one hand and pipes in the other. It had become an early morning ritual; it was the same way Jannie and Henri used to start each day onboard *De Ruyter*. "I wonder what happens?"

"No idea." Jannie laughed. "We'll be told what to do."

"Ja, and what about the Navy?" Henk looked serious. "Have you seen anything of them."

"Nee. I did meet a doctor who observed me while I was telling the colonel what had happened and why I'd panicked." He glanced at Henk. "I told him how it felt to see your home being bombed, de schijt we went through at Dunkirk. Henri, Dirk and all those soldiers." His fingers were trembling when he relit his pipe.

Henk was silent, his breathing faster.

"Lady Blackhurst was there too. It was good to talk to them. The doctor never said a word." He cleared his throat and spat on the ground beside him. "Miriam is better than any doctor and Ruth is better than any nurse." He smiled at Henk. "You are a very lucky man. You know that, don't you?"

"Ja, of course." Henk was nodding. "Sarah..." He paused, colouring slightly, "Sarah has asked me to marry her." He hurried on. "I was going to ask her, but I was too shy."

Jannie jumped up, grabbed Henk by his free hand and shook it vigorously. "You said yes?"

"I said yes." Henk was standing now, a broad smile on his face. "And now we must tell Miriam."

He suddenly stopped. "What did you do about the service?"

"What d'you mean?" Jannie was puzzled.

"You know. She is Jewish. I am Protestant." Henk looked worried.

"That's not a problem, Henk. They have an office for weddings like that. Mimi knows how it works." He nudged Henk, smiling broadly. "You'll have to decide what faith your children will be, though."

Looking anywhere but at Jannie, Henk blushed and walked on. He had not thought of that.

Sarah and Ruth were sitting at the kitchen table with Miriam when the men walked in. Jannie smiled and sat next to Mimi. "What are you looking so pleased about?" She glanced across at Henk, began to speak and fell silent.

Sitting between Ruth and Sarah, Henk put his hands on the table, tapped his fingers on it a couple of times, scratched his ear, coughed and looked helplessly at Sarah. After a long silence he whispered, "Have you said anything to Ruth?"

"No," Sarah whispered.

"What about?" whispered Mimi.

"Why are you whispering?" Ruth joined in.

"Because..." the women replied at the same time.

Jannie leant across and put his hand on Ruth's. "Because they have a big secret to tell you."

At which point, as Jannie expected, Ruth jumped onto Henk's lap, took his beard in both hands and shouted "Tell me!"

Henk tickled her ear with his beard before whispering into it, "Sarah and I are getting married."

Ruth pushed herself away so she could look into Henk's eyes. "Can I come?" Without waiting for his answer, she slipped off his knee and ran round to Sarah. "Can I come? Please?"

"Of course, my love. You can be my bridesmaid."

Later that day, when Mimi and Jannie were getting their supper ready, Mimi said, "We must tell Sam."

Jannie nodded.

"You miss him, don't you?" Pouring a couple of whiskies, Mimi took Jannie by the hand and led him into their sitting room.

"I miss him every day." Jannie put his arm round Mimi, pulled her closer and said quietly, "I have been wondering what he would say if we asked him to come here. There's plenty for him to do and we have the room."

"I wondered that too, my love." Mimi leant her head against his shoulder. "He'd be here with us, and Henk."

"He's met Sarah," Jannie told her. She laughed at his description of Sam's quick "It's kosher," when Sarah had asked about the pea and ham soup the first time she came onboard.

Mimi looked at Jannie's troubled expression. "What's worrying you?"

"I think Sam might say yes." He took a deep breath. "And, much as I want to, I think we would be wrong to ask him." He shifted so he could look at her and went on. "Sam has been with the Trevassos for nearly three months. He works hard and loves what he's doing and they like having him." He lit their cigarettes. "Mr T says he learns fast. And," inhaling a lungful of smoke, "there is Annie." He blew a smoke ring towards the ceiling.

"Perhaps we should give him the choice?" Miriam was playing Devil's advocate.

"Do you think so? I don't." Jannie went on. "Sam would do what he thinks is his duty. He would be torn between staying there and coming here." He sat up straight. "I think his duty is to the Trevasso family, not to us, though I would love him to be here."

Mimi took his hand. "Then we don't give him the choice. If he asks, if something happens, he can always come here." She picked up her glass. "We should drink to Sarah and Henk."

Chapter 26.

Jannie watched Adam working his horses as they traversed the field of wheat; the slow, majestic progress of Nelson, Anson and Rodney; the clatter of the reaper-binder, the endless flow of neatly bound sheaves. He could not watch for long. Collecting sheaves and standing them in stooks of three was a hot, tiring business. It was the first time he had worked on a farm.

The harvest had been underway since dawn. Because it had been showery the day before, they were anxious to get the last field cut today. There were many people from the village working comfortably alongside the Land Army girls; although he had only been there a couple of hours, Jannie was rather regretting he had offered to help.

Spotting Miriam walking across the stubble, he bent forwards and backwards to ease his knotted muscles and went to meet her. She took a bottle from her basket and, handing it to him, asked, "Had enough?"

"Ja." Jannie took a mouthful of cold tea. "Ah, that's better. Danke, my love." He offered her the bottle, saying, "I'm too old for this."

"You don't have to do it," Mimi chided. "The colonel doesn't expect you to work in the fields."

Hand in hand, they strolled over to the shade of the nearest hedgerow and sat down. "You're not too old," she laughed. "Look at Adam and those other ancients. It's just very different from what you're used to." She ran a hand through his dishevelled hair. "And you have to look after yourself." Mimi punched his arm lightly. "Here," she said, handing him his sketchbook and a pencil. "Draw me a picture of Adam and his horses."

While Jannie sketched, Miriam took her exercise book out of the basket and started writing. She had a few ideas about how children could learn their sums without effort, including the songs she used to sing with her mother. "Once two is two, two twos are four, the farmer's shut the door. Two threes are six, he's picking up some sticks. Two fours are eight, he's standing at the gate…"

She had not realised she was singing aloud until Jannie clapped his hands in delight. "I've never heard you singing, Mimi. You have a beautiful voice." He gazed at her. "Why don't you sing more often."

Miriam sighed. "I haven't sung that since the children died." She leant against Jannie. "I used to sing around the house. After Ike's death there wasn't much to sing about." She put her hand on his cheek. "Now you are here, the songs have come back."

Jannie leant towards her; the sound of the reaper was lost amid a sudden fusillade of shots and shouting.

"What?" Jannie and Miriam sprang to their feet, staring at the small stand of wheat in the middle of the field, now surrounded by men with guns and boys with sticks.

The ears at the top of the wheat were rippling with movement as scores of terrified rabbits sought a way to flee the ever-shrinking cover. Miriam turned away, appalled by the blood-lust in the faces of two boys as they cornered and beat a rabbit to death. Of those that escaped the ring of boys, most were shot by men further back.

Jannie stared in disbelief before swiftly gathering his jacket, picking up the basket and hurrying Miriam away. There was no escaping the noise.

Neither said anything on their way back to the cottage. Jannie stripped to the waist and washed himself at the kitchen sink. "Well," he said, pulling on a clean shirt, "that was not a pretty sight." He looked at Miriam, started to speak and thought better of it.

"What were you going to say?"

"It reminded me of what we heard from German refugees, Jews. About what happened when their neighbours turned on them. It was just like that. Sudden, shocking violence; trapped in town squares and streets, doors to their homes kicked in, shop windows smashed, the beatings; men and women shouting as they chased and punched and kicked them."

They did not hear Lady Blackhurst knock before she came in through the open back door. She heard Jannie's description, wincing when he said, "Seeing those rabbits trapped like that, the faces of those boys as they hit them, their eyes." He shook his head. "That is what Germans do to Jews."

"It's what happened when Ike got hit…" Miriam's voice trailed off when she saw Lady Blackhurst.

She and Jannie pushed back their chairs and started to get up.

"Please don't. I'm sorry to intrude."

Liz was turning to leave when Miriam recovered her poise. "Please join us."

There was a moment of awkward silence after Liz sat down. Jannie broke it. "This must happen on every farm." He saw her nod. "I had better write to Mr Trevasso and warn him. Sam heard the same stories."

"Yes, you must." Liz was saddened to see the misery on his and Miriam's faces. "It happens every year." Seeking to explain, she continued. "There are too many rabbits everywhere and they eat acres of corn. We shoot them all year round but it's impossible to keep the numbers down. This is one of the ways we try to control them."

"It was a shock to see it, milady." He sighed. "Jews, rabbits, vermin. It is hard for us to separate the way people behave, whatever the reason. Would those boys beat their neighbours to death if they thought they were vermin?" He looked at her. "Germans do."

"And English police." Miriam saw Liz start. "Some of them."

"I told you the other day, milady. Jews are an easy target. There are no countries that welcome them. Not even England." He looked steadily at her. "Except for you and a few others."

Chapter 27.

"That's a relief." Jannie handed the letter to Miriam. "It's from Frank."

She read it quickly, a smile lighting her face. "I'm so glad." Putting it back in its envelope, she looked up. "It was clever of him to send Sam off with Annie to catch fish."

They took their morning tea into the garden where they were soon joined by Sarah and Ruth. "The colonel's asked Henk to help him with the woods. The Ministry want to start felling some of the trees the other side of the road and he wants Henk to keep an eye on them." Sarah looked pleased. "It's good he's giving Henk more responsibility."

"It is," agreed Jannie. "I never thought of Henk as a landsman."

"I don't think he is," Sarah laughed, "but the colonel obviously does, and he's paying him." She danced a little jig, "He is giving us our future."

Whether she referred to God or the colonel was not clear to Jannie.

Chapter 28.

"Let's find Henk." Jannie hoisted Ruth onto his shoulders, called Sheba to heel and walked down to the river to find him.

"A woodsman now?" he called as he lifted Ruth down. "That's a big change."

"Ja." Henk laughed. "And much to learn." He knelt down. "I'll have to go to school with you, won't I?"

They walked towards the turbine house, Ruth and Sheba running ahead. "The colonel will help me." Henk looked serious. "The Ministry is sending their people to select and cut the timber they need. He is worried about that but cannot stop them. I think he hopes to save some of the older trees." He shrugged. "I have to tell him which of those they mark for cutting. I don't know what he hopes to do about that."

"This bloody war." Jannie lit a cigarette and smiled. "But without it you would not have met Sarah, and Mimi and I would not be married." Watching Ruth playing with Sheba, his face suddenly grim, "And her parents would not be missing her every minute of each day."

"We pray for them every night," Henk said quietly. "On our knees before she gets into bed."

"But…"

"But nothing," Henk cut him off. "We pray together for God to keep her Mutti and Papa safe. It is not much to ask." Henk looked at Jannie, "Is it?"

"Nee, my friend. It is not much." He flicked his cigarette butt into the river and watched it drift downstream before turning to Henk. "I hope He is listening."

Sheba came trotting back, Ruth close behind. Henk picked her up. "Let's show Jannie where we make electricity."

The quiet hum in the turbine house, the simplicity of the set up and the efficiency of the adjacent sawmill, impressed Jannie. "He is a far-sighted man, your colonel." Quietly, so Ruth could not hear, he added, "Sarah told us he is now paying you. I am so pleased, Henk."

Henk ducked his head, beaming with pleasure. "Me too." He looked up. "I never expected that. Or to be getting married." He paused. "The colonel does not think the Germans will invade. He said they could have destroyed the British and French armies at Dunkirk, crossed the Channel and landed in force. He does not think they could do so now."

"I hope he's right." Jannie looked doubtful. "I really do."

Checking that Ruth could not hear, Henk asked, "Do you know what the Navy is doing here?"

"Nee," Jannie shook his head. "We were told it is a Naval hospital but I do not believe that. The man I met didn't strike me as a doctor."

Henk laughed. "He's not. He was checking that you and Miriam are not spies. We met him when we arrived. I asked the colonel who he was, once I'd been here a few weeks."

Ruth wandered over, demanding attention. They shut the doors and walked back along the river bank, each man holding one of Ruth's hands and swinging her to and fro. The colonel, attracted by Sheba's barking, joined them, interested to learn what Jannie thought of his turbine house.

Henk and Ruth walked on when the two older men started talking about the technicalities. Sir Charles stopped and called after Henk, "I'm taking Jannie back now. See you at the office."

Walking away from the river, he asked, "Has Henk said anything to you about the hospital?"

"We were just talking about it." He looked at the soldier. "It is not our business what they do; we understand why you had us checked out." He laughed briefly. "I would have done the same."

The colonel smiled. "You and Henk are only here because Lady Teagle is very persuasive. And because the Admiral vouched for you."

Intrigued, Jannie did not have long to wait before he explained why.

"What I am about to tell you must only be shared with your wife and Henk. Understood?"

"Ja, milord."

"Good." He gestured towards his home. "It is true to say it is a convalescent hospital and that is how you must always describe it." He waited until Jannie nodded. "It is not sailors who are being made ready to return to battle. The Prime Minister wants to know what's needed to heal Europe."

"Christ." Jannie could not help himself.

The colonel looked at him. "I thought the same." He gave a grim smile. "The Germans beat us. We might have left most of our equipment behind when they drove us out, yet," he paused to look at the peaceful countryside, the river flowing through his fields, shook his head and continued, "yet those ruddy fools let us bring our men home. And now our Air Force is battling theirs and our Navy is ready to sink any ships that Hitler might use to invade. And," Sir Charles laughed aloud, "we have a secret weapon."

Jannie listened intently.

"A rogue, a maverick. A bloody-minded visionary called Churchill." Colonel Blackhurst slapped Jannie on the back. "Thank God."

"Have you heard him speak?" Without waiting for an answer, he continued. "Not only will we never surrender," he laughed, "but even now he is planning how to beat Germany."

Incredulous, Jannie asked, "Here?"

"Yes. Here. And we keep running our farm, 'patients' keep coming and going, the school will soon open its doors – and what goes on inside the 'hospital', my friend, is top secret."

And so it has remained until the publication of this book
(Editor's note)

Chapter 29.

As usual, Jannie and Miriam were waiting for the nine o'clock news. It was Sunday morning, 8th September. There was not a cloud in the clear blue sky and they were looking forward to going for a walk through the woods with Ruth, Sarah and Henk.

"This is the BBC Home Service. Here is the news." The radio crackled slightly.

"London's biggest and heaviest air raid ended just before five o'clock this morning, having lasted since half past eight yesterday evening."

"Mijn God," Jannie whispered, staring at the set, his face white, his voice trembling. Miriam was silent, tears running unheeded down her pale cheeks. She reached for Jannie's hand as the announcer continued.

"High explosive bombs of all sizes, and many incendiary bombs were dropped and scattered over large areas of the city – but it was the East End which bore the brunt of the attack."

They looked at each other, horror-struck.

"Many fires were started and at one time there were over four thousand fire-fighting appliances of one sort or another in use.

"The major fire was in the dock area and the glare from this, reflected in the smoke, could be seen all over the Metropolitan area."

Jannie turned the wireless off, his hand shaking as he fumbled for the knob. "Jesus."

Miriam's quiet sobs brought him swiftly to her side. "Come, my love." He half-lifted her to her feet and led her into the garden where he sat her gently on the bench. Lighting them each a cigarette, he sat beside her, put his arm around her and held her close. Neither spoke.

It was Sheba bounding up to them who drew them out of their shocked silence. "Where's your Missie?" whispered Jannie, stroking the puppy's soft ears. As Mimi eased herself upright to dry her tears, Ruth's little hand crept into hers. "Why are you crying?" she asked, before climbing onto Mimi's knees and staring intently at her. "Sarah's crying," she announced. "What did the man say?"

Jannie flicked his cigarette away and stroked Ruth's hair. "We are sad, little one. That's why people cry."

Ruth gazed at him steadfastly. "It is the War," she announced so solemnly that Jannie could not help but laugh.

"Yes, my dear. It is the War." And laughed again, thankful that she had never heard him swearing.

"We had better ring Wilkes Street."

Liz saw them coming. "You know where the phone is. I hope you can get through."

Relieved when Mrs Coward answered the phone and told her that everyone was safe, and that no bombs had fallen near her home, Mimi said, "You'd better call me when you can, my dear. You can always leave a message here. And don't forget to let me know if you need anything." She listened for a moment then laughed and hung up.

In answer to Liz's unasked question she said, "She wanted to know Hitler's address so she can send him the bill for repairs."

It was the start of fifty-seven days and nights of bombing raids on London. Other cities up and down the country were also heavily bombed. Casualties were appalling, indiscriminate destruction was widespread and the population bloodied – but unbowed.

Miriam and Jannie continued to listen to the news, wept when it was especially harrowing, and drew strength from each other, and from their regular correspondence with Sam.

Mimi felt completely safe with Jannie at her side. She found peace in singing and playing the piano, especially when playing for the children. Jannie drew strength from her quiet love and was at peace with himself when surrounded by children, or sketching around the farm.

Chapter 30.

"You look like a child in a toy shop." Miriam tugged Jannie's arm in vain as a gleaming traction engine huffed and puffed its way towards them, towing what he knew to be the threshing machine.

All hands had been busy for several days preparing for its arrival. Covers on ricks had been loosened, sacks tossed down from the barn loft to be shaken out and aired, any with holes to be repaired by Henk. Once the floor of the granary had been swept and bales of binder twine counted, all they had to do was grease the axles of the two carts, while Adam and Liz oiled the harnesses, and, with Sarah and Mimi's help, cleaned the brasses.

Ruth took Jannie to the smithy to help Will.

"Hello Ruth," Will twinkled, "Who is this?" he asked, gesturing towards Jannie.

"That's Jannie."

"Come to help, have ye?" He handed Jannie a broom and after pointing at the spiders' webs overhead and then at the floor, led Ruth to the woodshed to pick up the kindling as he chopped it.

It was a matter of moments to lay a fire in the forge. "Bellows," grunted Will as he lit the fire. Ruth blew out the match and stood back. It was obvious she had 'worked' here before. Jannie waited for Will's nod before pumping the bellows with his right foot.

It did not take long for the charcoal to catch.

Will sent Ruth to find Liz and tell her he was ready.

Jannie was astonished to see biggest horse he had ever seen being led by Liz into the smithy with Ruth perched on top. He lifted her off and went back to the bellows.

They were busy all morning. Old shoes removed, hooves cut and filed, Will's hammer ringing on the anvil, the hiss of hooves as hot new shoes were positioned before being nailed on, dogs milling underfoot scavenging bits of hoof – and all while the giant horses stood placidly, loosely tethered to a ring in the wall.

Old as he was, Will had no difficulty in lifting the huge, hairy feet of those shire horses and resting them on his knee as he bent to his task.

"Engineer's tea," Jannie said cheerfully, when Liz handed him the first of many mugs of black tea, brewed in a battered kettle kept steaming on the fire. He saw Will raise his bushy eyebrows and explained, "It was the same in my engine room."

Will said nothing as he went back to work. Liz was amused by the brief exchange; knew Jannie had sparked Will's interest and thought, *those two will get on.*

She led the last horse back to his stall with Ruth on his back, while Jannie helped Will shut up the smithy.

Getting onto his bike, Will nodded to Jannie. "I'll see you next time," as he slowly pedalled away.

Chapter 31.

A letter from Sam was waiting for them. Miriam propped it against the vase on the table while they washed their hands and faces.

"What a lovely morning." Mimi wondered how much sootier Jannie had looked when he was onboard *De Ruyter*, she saw a quiet contentment in his eyes.

"It was," he agreed. "I had no idea how to shoe a horse. Watching Will was a real eye-opener." He sat down. "And watching Ruth with those huge horses. I would not have been anywhere near them when I was that age."

They feasted on bread, cheese and mugs of beer before opening Sam's letter. "You read it, my dear." Jannie loved listening to Mimi's voice.

"Dear Jannie and Tante Mimi," she started then laughed. "Oh my word," she looked at Jannie, "They've finished threshing and now Sam is working on the traction engine." She put the letter down. "He was such a help when it arrived that Mr T told him he had better give the driver a hand while his mate's ill. There are only three more farms to do, so he won't be away long.'

"Does he say what he did, what it's like?" Jannie asked, leaning forward.

"Oh yes, in great detail." Mimi laughed. "You had better read it yourself. I don't know anything about steam engines." She looked fondly at Jannie. "He does say people from neighbouring farms come to help; they all bring beer and pasties; it's hot, dusty, dirty, noisy work; and great fun!"

He smiled, "We'll find out soon enough." And they did.

Chapter 32.

The school-room in the west wing was large, light and airy, its double doors opening onto the veranda and the tennis court beyond. The walls had recently been painted a warm yellow, with a brightly coloured alphabet running around the room on a frieze at Ruth's eye-height. As well as the required black-out curtains, the French doors and windows were hung with new nursery curtains decorated with images of children and animals, in the style of Mabel Lucy Atwell.

There was a round table with eight chairs in one corner, a pile of cushions in another, a huge sofa in the third and a blackboard and easel in the fourth. An upright piano stood by the door to the hall. There were children's story books, picture books, a large globe, wooden bricks and a range of toys and animals on the shelves and in the drawers of the large dresser, as well as chalk, paper, crayons and pencils.

"All set?" Lady Blackhurst asked Sarah.

"Oh yes." Sarah laughed, "Ready, willing and able." She danced around the room. "And six children coming tomorrow." She stood next to Liz, "And very nervous. I'm not a teacher."

"Nor am I," Liz reminded her, "but you've been practising with Ruth." She smiled. "I hope they all get on with each other."

By December they had twelve pupils, all under five. Their day started at nine o'clock with a mug of warm milk and a sing-song, either a nursery rhyme, a hymn or a folk-song. When not doing something together, they split into groups of four for the rest of the day. Indoor sessions usually lasted twenty minutes, once everyone had whatever they needed; unless it was cooking which always happened on Thursdays, when they all trooped off to the kitchen to make cakes or pies with Cook.

Music, dance, games, stories and drawing filled days when the weather was too bad to be outside. "Who's this school for," Mimi asked Sarah on one such day after watching Jannie showing four little boys a picture of a paddle boat before asking them to draw one. She had drifted quietly closer so she could hear what he was saying. "This is the one I used to work in," he told them. "Smoke comes out of the funnel like this, and the water behind the paddles is like mermaids' washing." He drew a couple of lines in the sky, "And this is a seagull. Like those white birds that follow the plough."

"What's a mermaid, Jannie?"

Mimi smiled and moved back to Sarah.

Sarah looked around the room. "Those little ones give more than they take without even knowing it." She nudged Mimi, "Don't they?"

Mimi hesitated before replying. "I never thought I could bear to be with children again, not after …" Her voice broke as tears welled up. She shook her head and blinked them away. "But now," she sighed, "I would be lost without them." She hugged Sarah. "I think you knew this would happen." Her "Thank you" was lost amid the laughter from children surrounding Liz on the cushions.

Clearing up at the end of the day, Sarah told Liz, "Some of the children have been asking if they can be angels or shepherds. Are we missing something?"

"Oh Lord," Liz laughed. "I thought we might get away without it."

"What?"

"Putting on a Nativity play."

Sarah frowned.

"Oh, sorry." Contrite, Liz explained. "The story of the birth of Jesus. Schools do a play every year; children love it."

She was surprised when Sarah said, "We've still got time," and laughed. "Ruth will love it."

Chapter 33.

That December it was as if the grim daily news of burning cities and mounting casualties was happening in another world. The children were oblivious and adults strove to hide their anxiety and fears.

"How are we going to do all this?" Sarah asked Liz, worrying about her wedding in two days' time as well as the prospect of putting on their Nativity play at such short notice.

"My dear, you really don't have to worry about your wedding. You know that." Sarah nodded. Thanks to Miriam and Sir Charles's visit to the Registry Office and another golden guinea, the marriage would take place in the school-room. The 'doctor' had agreed with Sir Charles that, as Henk had never been formally discharged from the Navy, it was indeed proper use of naval transport for a Wren to take the hospital's car to Andover to collect the Registrar and deliver him safely home after the service.

"It's a shame it can't be in our drawing room," Liz said wistfully, "That used to be such a lovely room."

"This is a lovely room," Sarah chipped in, "I wouldn't want to be married anywhere else…" she stopped and looked at Liz, "except at home." She gave her a crooked smile. "But I would never have met Henk if I'd stayed there."

Suddenly looking anxious, Sarah asked, "Are you sure it's a good idea to have it on a school day?"

Liz laughed. "It's a splendid idea. They will never forget it, and nor will you two." She pushed her out of the door. "Now go home. I'm sure you have things to do."

***

It was bright and breezy on Thursday 5th December. Henk lit the fire in the schoolroom at eight and, unusually, stayed on to help get the room ready.

An hour later Sarah greeted the children at the door. She helped them hang their coats, scarves and hats on their pegs before they sat down to drink their milk.

"Listen, my dears, we have a surprise for you."

When their chatter died away Miriam continued. "Sarah and Henk are getting married today." Ruth jumped out of her chair, squeaking with delight; a few of the other girls and boys joined her. The others stared at them, eyes wide and mouths open. Clapping her hands, Miriam quickly restored order.

"We are getting married here," a smiling Sarah told them. "We want you all to come to the party."

As Liz predicted, it was a lovely wedding. The children sang sweetly, Cook surpassed herself, music and laughter filled the room and Ruth was the perfect bridesmaid.

Adam drove Sarah and Henk away in the trap, freshly cleaned, polished and decorated with coloured ribbons. Sir Charles had many friends among the neighbouring landowners, one of whom lent the newly-weds a warm and well-appointed cottage not far away.

"Come on, meisje." Jannie scooped up the yawning Ruth and carried her back to his and Miriam's home. This was the first time she had been away from Sarah and Henk and they were anxious to ensure she felt secure and loved.

They need not have worried. "It was like having a little shadow," Mimi told Sarah and Henk when they returned. "We loved having her."

Chapter 34.

"Do you think we should tell the children about Hannukah?" Sarah asked Miriam as they were tidying up after school next day.

"What's that?" Liz was intrigued.

"Oh," Sarah looked surprised, "it's when we celebrate the miracle of the oil." She told Liz about the return of the Maccabees to the Temple and how they only had enough oil for one day but somehow it lasted until they had made some more eight days later.

"That's why some call it the Festival of Lights. We light a candle every day, one for each of the eight days."

"And that's why Jannie made them the menorah," Mimi joined in. Liz had admired the distinctive candlestick with its nine candle holders when Henk and Sarah opened their wedding presents.

"Will is a good teacher," Jannie told them. "Patient too." He smiled at Liz. "And he corrected my mistakes."

"It starts next week, on the 14th," Sarah told Liz, "and ends on the 21st. Your Christmas is on the 25th, isn't it?"

"Yes." Liz looked thoughtful. "I was thinking of having our Nativity play on the 18th. It's a Wednesday and would be a good way to end the term." She sighed. "I can't ask you to help with that. They don't go together, do they?"

"Listen Liz," Sarah took her hand. "We have met with nothing but kindness since we came to your country. You welcomed us into your home when we had nowhere to go. Gave us work. Jannie and Miriam too. Our beliefs may be different but we worship the same God. I don't think He will mind if we celebrate life and light together."

With that settled, they sat down to devise a simple Nativity play. It was, they soon discovered, easier said than done.

Having heard Henk singing 'Silent Night' to Ruth, Liz suggested he opened the play with a solo. "He could start singing it with the children in the hall, as a processional carol once everyone's seated."

"He'll never do that," Jannie said quietly to Miriam.

"He will," she whispered, "He'll do anything for her."

Henk also said he would teach the children to dance a simple hornpipe, though Liz was not sure how that fitted into a Nativity play.

With much to do, and little time in which to do it, Liz roped in the Land Army girls to help Adam prepare and decorate the two hay wains they would use to fetch the children and their families from the village.

Sarah and the others soon had the children happily dancing, singing and learning their parts. It was a joyous if chaotic time amid nightly reminders of the War, as Germany continued to rain bombs on cities, reported in sombre tones each morning on the nine o'clock news.

One morning, Liz told Miriam she was wanted on the telephone. Jannie went with her to take the call. They feared the worst, for there had been another savage air raid on London's East End.

"What? Speak up, this is a terrible line." Miriam looked strained and anxious as she struggled to hear the voice at the other end. Her "Oh, Mrs Edelman. Are you alright?" drew Jannie to her side.

Putting her hand over the mouthpiece, she whispered, "She's alright," then closed her eyes to concentrate on Mrs Edelman's words before replacing the handset with a loud sigh and turning to lean against Jannie.

He held her in silence, feeling her tension drain away. "Let's go outside. We could both do with a cigarette."

"Mrs Edelman said to tell you they felt very safe in your shelter and to thank you for making it so comfortable." She laughed. "And said next time you're round could you add a couple more bunks."

"What about your house? Is that alright?"

"Oh yes." Miriam smiled at a memory, "She reckons a guardian angel lives there. None of the bombs landed near it, though Number 2 was burnt down by an incendiary."

"That was close enough." Jannie hugged her. "What about their homes?"

"Still standing." Mimi shook her head in wonder. "She is taking it all in her stride. She said they are so busy they're open all the time. Lots of firemen come in after their shifts, sit down with a mug of tea and fall asleep.

She lets them stay there as long as possible. A few off-duty nurses come, as well as all the regulars." She looked at Jannie. "I hope Sam is safe. Mrs E says they've been bombing Cornwall."

"We would have heard if anything had happened." Jannie reassured her with a hug. "We had better get back to the children."

Chapter 35.

Because some of the school children were evacuees, Sarah and Liz decided to make all the costumes and props themselves, ably helped by the others. That way, no-one would be left out. Old dressing up boxes, the linen cupboard and attic had been raided; the colonel lent walking sticks and a shepherd's crook; Jannie and Henk discovered hidden talents with cardboard, glue and paint; and Cook provided goose feathers for the angels' wings.

School days were taken up with rehearsing the simple play, practising the three carols and making costumes. Henk's hornpipe had been quietly dropped. Jannie was surprised by the children's ready acceptance of the parts they had to play and their enthusiasm for dressing up.

"He must have had a very different childhood," Sarah commented one evening when she and Miriam were tidying up.

"The only person he talks to about himself is Ruth, and only if I'm out of earshot," Mimi replied.

"He'll tell you when he's ready. Henk's the same." Sarah laughed. "We've married a couple of strangers."

"It's the War!" they chorused.

"Thank goodness it's dry." That sentiment echoed around Saffron House as Wednesday morning dawned cold, but clear.

Henk lit the schoolroom fire early and went with Liz to ready the wagons. They had prepared the schoolroom the evening before. A couple of the 'hospital' staff had carried in extra chairs and stayed to help move furniture. The costumes had been completed by Sarah and Miriam with help from three of the naval 'nurses', and the 'doctor' asked if some of their 'patients' could attend.

"Perfect." Sarah clapped her hands, amazed, joyful and nervous. The schoolroom had been transformed by a few simple props and careful positioning of lights. A stable, an inn door and a hillside awaited the cast, their costumes hanging neatly over the backs of twelve chairs.

"Listen, my dears." Sarah clapped her hands for silence. "Do you remember what we are going to do this morning?"

Twelve hands shot up.

"Yes Andrew?"

"Collect ivy."

"Anything else? Yes Maureen?"

"Decorate the Missmus tree."

Jannie and Miriam took the little ones into the woods to fetch the ivy Henk had stripped off trees the day before. Meanwhile Henk carried the Christmas tree into the entrance hall and secured it in a freshly polished brass bucket.

The morning passed in a whirl of activity. After a noisy school dinner, the children were wrapped in rugs and soon fast asleep on their big cushions as the wagons departed to fetch their parents and guardians.

The school room was full. People from the village, together with the estate staff and a few 'hospital' staff, sat entranced as angels sang, shepherds watched their sheep and no room could be found in the inn.

Children and adults rejoiced together in the story of Christmas and prayed for peace on earth.

All too soon it was over.

"Thank you, God." Liz raised her eyes to the heavens as she flicked the reins over the horses' backs and followed Adam's wagon down the drive. Children and adults waved as the wheels crunched on the gravel. Someone started singing and soon everyone joined in, the strains of 'Silent Night' gradually fading into the distance.

"Didn't they look beautiful?" Miriam wiped away a tear, moved by the memory of the children's glowing faces peering over fronds of ivy and brightly coloured ribbons woven around the sides of the wagons.

"Ja." Henk and Sarah were waving to Ruth. She had insisted on helping Adam and was now snuggled up beside him as he drove away. A picture of her standing alone onboard *De Ruyter*, tears streaming down her cheeks, flashed before Henk's mind's eye, together with a sudden thought for the agony of her parents. He kissed Sarah before whispering, "Her poor parents. Please God, keep them safe." They stayed outside for a moment, lost in their shared memory of that dreadful night, before joining the others.

Back inside, Jannie was too engrossed in making a quick sketch of the departing wagons to notice the colonel watching discreetly over his shoulder. He had moved away by the time Jannie put his pencil and sketch-book in his pocket and joined the others by the fire.

"Time to square away."

Henk smiled. Mimi was beginning to sound like a sailor.

They soon tidied the room, raked the fire and made sure the screen was firmly in place. "No more school till after Christmas." Looking pensive, Miriam walked slowly over to the piano.

Henk asked, "Do you know 'Ik Hou Van Holland'?" He translated "I love Holland." and hummed a few bars. As Miriam picked out the tune Henk and Jannie started singing, their deep bass and tenor voices soon joined by Miriam and Sarah singing the chorus. The colonel came in, unnoticed until he applauded at the finish.

"The wagons are coming back. Would you like to sing them home?"

Thus started a new Christmas tradition at Saffron House, one that continues to this day.

Chapter 36.

Christmas in Cornwall

It was still dark when Mr Trevasso opened the door. "Wake up Sam, it's Christmas Day, when the morning stars sang together, and all the sons of God shouted for joy." He looked at the sleepy boy. "Get dressed, we're getting the cows in early."

Milking over, Annie fed the chickens and pigs while Mr T turned the cows out and Sam hosed down the milking parlour.

Mrs T made breakfast.

Whistling Aggie to heel, Sam set off on her morning walk, as he did every day. And, as he did every morning and evening, he stood for a few minutes, eyes closed, while he communed silently with his family. Opening his eyes and raising them to the stars, now fading as the sky lightened, he whispered, "I love you, Mutti, Papa. I love you, Rachel."

When Aggie came bouncing up to him, he picked her up and buried his tear-streaked face in the nape of her neck. Setting her down, boy and dog raced home.

"Come on Sam," Annie patted the seat beside her as her parents climbed into the back of the trap; all were warmly dressed against the biting wind. Sam tugged his hat down to stop it blowing away as Annie set off along the farm track and up the hill to the chapel.

She slowed Janet to a walk on entering the town, taking care to avoid the many people heading the same way. "Where do they all live?" Sam asked her.

"It's a big place," she replied, "And lots work in the mines." She looked at him, "You never see them usually."

While Annie hitched Janet's reins to a gate-post, Sam helped Mrs T climb down from the trap. Mr T put his hand on Sam's shoulder as he jumped down and left it there. "Don't be nervous, lad." He gave a friendly squeeze. "Just do what we do and don't forget to mouth the words when we're praying and singing."

He touched Sam's cap; "And take this off." Sam grinned. "Aye, aye sir."

The chapel was warm and full. Sam was surprised at the number of people crowded in and amazed by the singing. With Mrs T surreptitiously nudging him when it was time to sit, stand or kneel, Sam navigated his way carefully through the service without mishap. While Mr and Mrs Trevasso chatted to the minister and some of their friends, Annie and Sam slipped away to unhitch the trap.

"What did you think of that?" Annie asked, curious to know Sam's reaction to a Christian service.

"Different," he replied enigmatically. "Very different." He looked at her, a wicked glint in his laughing eyes, "Now I know why we make the women go upstairs."

"What?" Annie did not know that Jewish men and women were kept apart during their services. "Why's that?"

"Because you distract us." Sam did not elucidate and her parents arrived before she had time to ask what he meant. Sam was glad of that. He had not meant to be so honest.

"Home, James, and don't spare the horses." Mr T laughed and slapped Sam on the back. "That wasn't too bad, was it?"

"Nee, meneer, not too bad. Just different."

As soon as they arrived home, Mrs T and Annie bustled inside to get Christmas dinner ready. Aggie bounded out, barking excitedly as Mr T unhitched Janet and led her to her stable. She raced around the yard while Sam pushed the trap into its shed before calling her to heel. "Come, Aggie. Here." She jumped into his arms and nuzzled under his chin as he hugged her. "It was very strange," he whispered, "I don't know what Mutti would say." The sight of so many families sitting together, the hum of conversation, people looking around to smile and wave to their friends had reminded Sam how far away he was from all whom he loved.

Seeing how forlorn Sam looked, Mr T went inside. "I'll take over here," he told Annie. "Go and get Sam." When she had gone, he said, "He needs cheering up."

"Poor boy," Mrs T agreed. "I can't imagine what it must be like not knowing how your family are." She turned from the stove, "We're all he has, us and the Jansens." She stirred the gravy. "They must be feeling the same."

Mr T put his arm round his wife's waist. "He's a good lad. Works hard. Kind too." He gave her a peck on the cheek. "Happy Christmas, my dear."

Martha put the spoon down, wiped her hands on her apron, put them around Frank's neck and kissed him, a long, loving kiss. "Happy Christmas, Frank," she whispered, before pushing him away. "We don't want to give the children ideas."

Frank laughed. "I don't think they need any help from us."

He was right. Finding Sam leaning against the trap and cuddling Aggie, Annie crept up behind him, put her hands over his eyes and murmured, "Guess who?"

She felt his shoulders rise as he tensed, before relaxing and leaning back against her. Annie slipped her arms around him and rested her head against his. After a while Sam put Aggie down. Annie let go of him as he turned and smiled hesitantly. "It's time to go in."

Sam cleared his throat. "Ja, danke. Er, thank you." He did not meet her eye.

Annie smiled to herself, *you really are rather sweet.* "Come on," she said, and took his hand.

It might have been the second Christmas of the War, but a visitor to Nanjigga Farm would never have thought the country was subject to strict food rationing.

Once they had cleared the table and done the washing up, Mr T turned the wireless on. "It's nearly time for the King's Speech," he told Sam. "He addresses the Empire every Christmas."

The family stood as the National Anthem filled the room. They sat quietly during the long, static-filled silence before the King's first words: *"In days of peace the feast of Christmas is a time when we all gather together in our homes, young and old, to enjoy the happy festivity and goodwill which the Christmas message brings…"*

Sam bowed his head as the King went on, *"War brings, among other sorrows, the sadness of separation…"* Mr Trevasso put his arm round Sam's shoulders when the King asked, *"how many more children are there here who have been moved from their homes to safer quarters?"* There was not a dry eye around the table as he went on, *"To all of them, at home and abroad, who are separated from their fathers and mothers, to their kind friends and hosts, and to all who love them, and to parents who will be lonely without them, from all in our dear island I wish every happiness that Christmas can bring."* Sam raised his head and squared his shoulders at the King's rallying call, *"Remember …by facing hardship and discomfort cheerfully and resolutely not only do they do their own duty, but they play their part in helping the fighting Services to win the War."*

He heard little of the rest of his speech, save for his hope *"to make the world a better place and life a worthier thing."*

***

The family sat as the last bars of the National Anthem faded and the wireless was switched off, each lost in thought. Mrs T was the first to speak. "That poor man." Sam looked at her. "How he manages to read that I'll never know." Seeing the boy's puzzled expression, she went on, "He has a terrible stutter."

Sam did not know, nor did he know what 'stutter' meant until Annie demonstrated, and, much to everyone's relief, gave such an astonishing performance that they were soon reduced to helpless laughter.

"That was very cruel," her father chided.

"B-b-but v-v-very f-f-f-f-funny," countered Sam, thereby rekindling their mirth until Mrs T stood up and restored order with her brisk commands. "Put the kettle on, Sam. Cups and saucers, Annie. Father, fetch the presents."

"Is there time to take Aggie for a quick walk?"

"Yes. Don't be long." Mrs T watched as Sam hurried out, his puppy at his heels. "Poor kid," she muttered, "he looks so lost."

"Shall I go after him?" Annie asked, having set out the tea things on the table. "Yes, quick as you can." As Annie opened the door she called after her, "And don't you be teasing him."

Annie shook her head and ran out.

When he heard Annie calling, Sam stopped. "Race you," she laughed, not giving him time to reply as she sped past him. Annie leant against the gate as he panted up to her. "Hah!" he grinned, "That's the only way you can beat me." He gave her a gentle nudge. "Isn't it?"

"Was that awful?" Annie asked, suddenly serious.

"What?" Sam was confused.

"Today, all of it." Annie looked at him. "Chapel, Christmas dinner, the King's speech." She put a hand on his arm. "Everyone with their families." Her voice dropped. "Everyone but you?"

Sam looked at her hand, aware of the weight of it. He looked at Annie. "The King…" He took a deep breath, "The King made me sad, very sad." He shook his head. "I have not been away from my…" His voice quavered. "My family." Straightening up, he looked at Annie. "I miss them all the time." He tapped her hand lightly. "But I am happy here." He nodded towards the farm. "Your Mutti and Papa are good people." Leaning towards her, smiling, he whispered so quietly she had to lean forwards to hear what he said, "And you," he paused, "are very…" he paused again. "You can't run as fast as me." And raced off. Laughing and panting, the two of them burst into the kitchen, Aggie jumping and barking at their heels. A pile of carefully wrapped parcels stood on the sideboard.

They opened them after tea, each admiring the gifts they had received and those of the others. Most admired was Jannie's framed portrait of *De Ruyter* steaming up the River Lek. Speechless, Sam could only hold it at arm's length, staring at his old ship until Mr T asked if he could see it. Most coveted, at least by Annie, was Miriam's gift of a pocket Kodak Vest Camera, complete with two rolls of film.

Sam said, "I am very happy here, mevrouw, thank you," and gave Mrs T the pot of violets he had carefully nurtured in a warm, sheltered corner of the garden, along with a welcome bottle of Yardley's Lavender Water, blushing when she hugged him. Then he handed Mr T a beautifully wrapped package. The farmer shook it lightly before untying the string and carefully removing the paper. He was not surprised to find a tin of Player's Navy Cut, but was intrigued by a second, much heavier cardboard box. His eyes gleamed when he lifted the lid. "Thank you, Sam. It's just what I need." Taking out the black-handled jack-knife, he was surprised to find a lanyard coiled beneath it. Pulling it out, he examined the two neatly spliced loops. "Did you make these?"

"Ja, meneer, so you don't lose the knife," he grinned.

Finally, Sam picked up a slender package, blushing as he handed it to Annie. Annie opened it on her lap giving a loud gasp when she discovered a pair of handsome leather gloves. She slipped them on, delighted by their warmth and how well they fitted. Holding up her hands, she wiggled her fingers, beaming with pleasure. "Not for farming," Sam cautioned.

"Of course not." Annie's smile was warm. "They're beautiful. Thank you."

"And that is so you don't forget," Sam laughed as she found a pocket diary still in the wrapping paper.

"This is from us both," Mrs T told Sam, handing him a bulky parcel, which contained a beautifully knitted blue sweater. "It's called a Guernsey," she said, as he pulled it on.

"Oh mevrouw, danke. Er, thank you; Meneer, thank you." He puffed out his chest. "So smart."

"Wear it to work, Sam. It's to keep you warm."

"I will," he promised.

"And this." `Annie joined in, giving him a small, squashy parcel.

"Perfect!" Sam held up the grey tweed cap and put it on at a jaunty angle. "Danke, Annie. It is very warm. Can I wear it to work?"

"Of course."

Annie jumped up to show Sam the ear flaps. "And pull these down when it's windy."

It was Sam's first Christmas; his only happy one.

Chapter 37.

Hampshire

It was not until he started to draw *De Ruyter* that Jannie recalled how the Admiral's Flag Lieutenant had described watching her arrive on her last voyage up the Medway that calm May night: "by the struggling moonbeam's misty light." How he had heard the funereal metallic note of her damaged paddle before the battered ship came limping past, steam and smoke from the many bullet holes in her funnel obscuring the river bank and dimming her broad white wake; then seeing her bridge, stripped of it wheelhouse, the black shapes of her two Lewis guns, their gunners and the captain clearly visible. He made two pencil sketches before he was satisfied with his composition. Taping a large piece of cartridge paper to his drawing board, he worked swiftly, lightly sketching his chosen outline before switching to pen, brush and ink. So vivid was the picture in his mind that he scarcely looked at his sketches. Swift, assured pen strokes were followed by confident sweeps of the different brushes he used; pausing occasionally to stand back, squinting at the paper as the picture took shape; darting forward to add a stroke here, a line there until, exhausted, he laid down his brush. He stood back, looked at the picture and relaxed.

Muttering, "It is finished," he went to find Henk, closing the door carefully behind him.

"You look worn out." Mimi was worried until she saw him smile.

"I am, my love, but I think it was worth it." He looked at his ink-stained hands and laughed. "This won't scrub off."

Jannie made Henk stand by the door while he turned on a standard lamp adjacent to the drawing board. "Come." Jannie stood aside so Henk could see the picture. "Mijn God!" Henk looked shocked. He looked at Jannie. "How did you see this?"

"Not me. It was Flags. He told me." Jannie explained.

"All this is ink?" Henk looked at the empty pots, the brushes and pens in jam jars filled with black water, and Jannie's stained hands and clothes.

"Ja. It does not need much colour, a little red in the corner of the sooty ensign, a touch of yellow for the moon, a little more at the bottom of the funnel." He looked at Henk, "We meant to paint it grey before we sailed, but there was no time."

"It would not have made any difference." Henk was emphatic. "It was filthy by then." He stood back to study the painting.

"Remarkable." Henk looked again "No, it is outstanding." He was lost for words. "It is for Miriam, ja?"

"Ja, and a book of drawings." Jannie looked critically at his painting. "I have to get it mounted and framed."

"Don't forget to sign it," Henk smiled. "That is a truly magnificent painting." He thought for a moment. "You must have it copied. Milord would like a copy; Flags too. So would I."

Unknown to Jannie, Colonel Blackhurst had contacted Kenneth Clark, a fellow member of his London club, about the talented Dutch artist who was now living on his estate. Mr Clark, head of the War Artists' Advisory Committee, added Jannie's name to his list and told the Colonel to let him know if Mr Jansen ever needed any help.

Thus it was that five signed copies were made of Jannie's painting, now titled *After Dunkirk*. Such was its impact on all who saw it that other unsigned copies were sent by the Advisory Committee to editors of newspapers in London and New York, attributed at Jannie's insistence, to 'An Unknown Artist.' Jannie continued painting and drawing, blissfully unaware that his work was acclaimed around the world.

Fourteen years later, Peter Teagle looked at his father's copy hanging prominently in the study of their Hampshire home. It was extraordinary how that old engineer had captured the moment without having even seen it. He made a note to call on the Reverend Henley, one-time flag-lieutenant to his father, and ask him what he remembered of the occasion.

A couple of days before Christmas Jannie was in the forge, wire-brushing the menorah he was making for Miriam. "Nearly finished?" Henk's voice made him jump.

"Ja, final touches now, then a little oil and lot of polishing." He placed the candlestick on the anvil and stood back. "Tea?" When Henk nodded, he pumped the bellows three of four times to makes the coals glow before putting a blackened kettle on top.

Henk laughed. "I miss our engineer's tea."

Jannie filled two mugs and offered Henk a cigarette.

"Danke." They smoked and drank their tea in companionable silence. Flicking his cigarette butt into the fire, Henk said, "I'm going to the midnight service on Christmas Eve." He looked at Jannie, "Will you come with me?"

"Huh," Jannie had not expected that. Realising his dear, imperturbable shipmate was nervous, he answered, "Yes. It will do me good."

Ruth had learnt enough about Christmas from her school-friends to know that Father Christmas came down the chimney and that children hung out empty seaboot stockings for him to fill. "There's little harm in that." Sarah and Miriam were mulling over what to do about this Christian feast.

"Nor in making paper-chains and giving presents," Miriam agreed. "There's little enough joy in the world."

"Has Jannie said anything about going to church?"

"No," Miriam laughed, "He's a good man, but not very religious."

Hiding her surprise when he told her he was going with Henk, Miriam gave Jannie a hug. "Do you want me to come with you?"

"No, my love," Jannie gazed at her, "I think maybe Henk is missing Henri and wants to talk about him." He wrapped his arms around her. "It will be good if he does. Good for me too."

They were silent, eyes closed, each drawing strength from the other. Eventually she opened her eyes, sighed a little and whispered, "This damned war."

Jannie placed a hand gently beneath her chin, raised her head and replied, "This damned war brought us together, my dear, for which I thank God daily."

Miriam smiled and closed her eyes again as she kissed him.

Ruth ensured that this Christmas was special. Having absorbed the excitement of her friends at school, she dragged Henk and Jannie off to search the woods for holly, yet more ivy, and mistletoe. Equally demanding of Sarah and Miriam, she carefully cut strips from the newspaper pages she had messily painted on the kitchen table, before gluing them into paper chains.

Henk cut a branch from a sycamore tree and mounted it in a block of wood which he placed in a corner of their sitting room, ready to decorate on Christmas Eve. Never has a tree been decorated with more enthusiasm and less skill than theirs.

Christmas was always special to these two refugee families.

Chapter 38.

The colonel stood in the school-room door one bitterly cold February morning and beckoned to Sarah. Telling her six pupils to draw pictures of their homes, she left with him. "Sorry to drag you away, my dear, but there's someone coming later this morning I'd like you and the others to meet."

"And the children?" she asked.

"No, just their teachers. Liz and Cook will look after the little ones." The colonel looked at his watch and said, "I'll be back in an hour," as he hurried away.

They had not expected to find an equally curious Henk in the hall when the colonel summoned them. "Before we go in, you must promise me never to breathe a word of this to anyone." They had never seen Colonel Blackhurst so serious. Having received their assurances, he went on. "What you don't know, and I apologise for not telling you before, is that everything you and I are doing here is an elaborate cover for a most secret organisation." He looked at them. "I know you realised the hospital is not what it seems. Once it had been established, and once Henk, Sarah and Ruth arrived, having a school alongside a working farm gave us the simplest and most effective cover possible. The icing on the cake was when Lady Teagle asked us to take in Jannie and Miriam." He smiled. "All your references are impeccable. And, since you arrived, you have earned my complete trust."

He looked at them for a moment, noting how his guests seemed to be standing taller.

"Come." He turned and led them through the west wing and into the library of the House. "Make yourselves at home, I'll be back in a minute."

"Curiouser and curiouser," Miriam said quietly as she looked at Henk. "What were you doing this morning?"

"Working in the saw-mill." He grinned, "Warm work and dry." They fell silent as the door opened.

Mr Churchill bustled in, closely followed by Colonel Blackhurst. The plump, bald man in a dark suit and signature bow tie came up to the small group. "Couldn't come here without meeting the rogues who pinched a paddle-boat from under the nose of the Nazis."

He laughed, "And dumped a load of Jews in Admiral Teagle's lap."

"I was one," Sarah whispered as she reached for Henk's hand. "They saved our lives."

"So they did, my girl, so they did." Churchill studied her. "I am glad…"

He was about to say more when Jannie interrupted, gazing sternly at the Prime Minister. "They are all Dutch, milord."

Churchill looked with interest at the man who stood before him. "Ah, Engineer Jansen. I have heard of you." He paused for a long moment before laughing. "Your friend, Henri, sent me a box of cigars."

Suddenly serious, he continued, "And then you took your ship to Dunkirk. Why did you do that?"

"It was our duty, sir." Jannie's simple answer hung in the silence that followed.

No one ever forgot the tears filling the eyes of the Prime Minister. "Your duty." He blew his nose. "It cost him his life."

"And the others." Henk's low rumble reminded him.

"Yes, and the others." Churchill looked around him. "You brought several thousand men home, but the price was high."

So quietly that they had to strain to hear him, he told Jannie, "The price is always too high," turned and left.

Chapter 39.

The Blitz ended on the night of May 10th, 1941. By the time the last bomber departed in the early hours of that morning, over 700 tons of high explosive and 2,393 incendiary bombs had been dropped in the most intensive air-raid of all the many raids on London.

Miriam was amazed her home had not been destroyed and delighted that the synagogue had remained open throughout. Two weeks later she and Jannie wept when they heard the news that *HMS Hood* had been sunk. The sinking of the *Bismark* two days after was small consolation for the great loss of life.

***

"This looks interesting," Liz said as she handed a buff envelope to Jannie.

Jannie's eyebrows rose as he read the letter. Placing it with great care in front of Miriam, he stuttered, "Read this."

She read it silently, read it again and handed it back.

Much the same reaction was being played out in Henk's home and at Nanjigga Farm.

Jannie had been commanded by the Admiralty to attend Buckingham Palace at ten o'clock on Wednesday 25th June, to receive, on behalf of his relatives, the Distinguished Service Cross awarded posthumously to Temporary Lieutenant Henri Kuiper Royal Navy.

Henk and Sam were invited to attend. They were not to know it was unusual for people who were not relatives to be invited to these occasions, nor that it was exceptional for three from one ship to be present. Lady Teagle had many friends in extraordinary places, one of whom had briefed Queen Wilhelmina.

After a flurry of letters to and from Cornwall, Miriam booked hotel rooms near Paddington Station; their travel warrants arrived and Henk and Jannie cleaned and pressed their uniforms. Mrs T took Sam into Penzance to buy a dark grey lounge suit, white shirt, tie and black shoes, his birthday presents from Tante Mimi and Jannie. She also made him have his hair cut.

Jannie looked at the bronzed young man in a smart suit hurrying towards him. "Sam?" Recognising his smile, he flung his arms out wide to embrace the boy. "My God, you have changed."

The joy of those three sailors was a welcome sight to the war-weary passengers hurrying to catch their trains. London was very different from the city they had left a year ago. Shells of burnt-out buildings were propped up by great baulks of timber and there were many gaps where houses had been bombed; uneven pavements, busy with pale, strained-looking people, added to the hazards of negotiating unaccustomed traffic. It was a surreal contrast to the rural life to which they were accustomed and a relief to sink into the shabby armchairs in the lounge of their hotel, cups of tea in their hands as they chatted away.

Sam brought them back to earth. "What will happen if Hitler beats Russia?"

"It's only been three days since they attacked," Jannie reminded him. "He cannot beat Russia. No-one can. It's too big." He tapped Sam on the knee. "You know what happened to Napoleon?"

"Ja, he was beaten by the winter."

"And Hitler will inevitably be beaten by the winter." Jannie's emphatic reply convinced Sam, who turned to Henk to tell him about Aggie.

As Henk and Jannie were much more interested in Annie, Sam was steered gently into telling them all about his life at Nanjigga Farm, from which they easily deduced the boy was more interested in the girl than his work. Satisfied he was being treated kindly, and knowing that affairs of the heart were none of their business, they sallied forth to find somewhere to eat.

Receiving Henri's Distinguished Service Cross from the hand of King George was an experience like no other in Jannie's long life. "He asked me to thank Henri's family when we go home, as if he knows we will win the war." He looked bemused. "Where does he get his strength from?"

"His faith." Henk's simple answer was clear and unequivocal.

Before they could ask him what else the King had said, a young Dutch lieutenant approached and, with an "Excuse me, gentlemen, please follow me," ushered them to an elegant side room.

It took them a moment to recognise the woman standing by the window as their Queen. Instantly coming to attention, Jannie and Henk bowed their heads, quickly followed by Sam. It was a brief meeting during which Her Majesty asked about their escape, thanked them for taking *De Ruyter* to Dunkirk and offered her sympathy and condolences for the deaths of Henri and Dirk. She asked Sam what he was doing in Cornwall and, having listened carefully to his stumbling reply, turned to Jannie.

"Engineer Jansen," her voice regal, "In recognition of your gallant actions and your leadership, I am pleased to present you with the Bronze Cross." Taking the medal from the lieutenant, she pinned it to Jannie's uniform and shook his hand.

Moving away from Jannie, she commanded quietly, "Meneer Bakker, come here please."

Blushing and hesitant, Henk stepped forward. "Meneer Bakker, for your undoubted courage and skill in the same action, I am pleased to present you with the Orange Order." Having pinned the medal to his uniform and shaken his hand, she went up to Sam. "Thank you, young man, our country is grateful to you." She took a gold and enamelled brooch in the form of the Dutch flag and gave it to him, saying "Wear this with pride."

And then she was gone.

The lieutenant escorted them through the Palace. At the door he told them, "Her Majesty was delighted to meet you. She has heard all about your adventures." He smiled as he said to Sam, "Look after that brooch; it was given to her by her father."

At the door, he shook their hands and saluted. "It has been an honour to meet you gentlemen."

They stopped outside the palace gates, Jannie to have a cigarette while Henk lit his pipe. Sam watched a sailor having his photograph taken. Noticing he gave his details as he paid, he hurried over to ask the photographer to take their picture.

"Well done, jonge." Jannie looked at his watch and was surprised it was only 1130. "Let's have lunch." Sam's train left at 1400 and he wanted to make sure Sam caught it.

Traction engines were discussed thoroughly as they ate, comparisons were made between sea and river fishing, the antics of puppies brought tears of laughter, and Henk and Jannie learnt more about Annie.

All too soon the train was pulling slowly out of the station, Sam's eyes watering as he leant out of the window waving to Jannie and Henk.

"It's a shame he couldn't come with us," Henk said as the train disappeared.

"Ja, for us," Jannie agreed, "But he never said anything about that."

"Would you," Henk chuckled, "with Annie waiting for you?" He looked at Jannie. "What's she like?"

Jannie shrugged, "She is good for him. That is what matters." He glanced at Henk, "She is a good worker, bright, lively and full of laughter." He remembered seeing her galloping across the fields and jumping a gate. "Brave too."

"And is she good looking?" Henk was curious.

"Ye-es." Jannie hesitated. "She is graceful, slender, but I wouldn't say beautiful. Not like a film star." He laughed. 'More like a warm, sunny day; she has a lovely smile, just like her mother."

"Lucky boy."

"I don't think he knows it, Henk." Jannie looked at him. "D'you remember your first girl-friend?

"Of course I do." Henk beamed. "I married her."

"Sarah? Truly?"

Henk laughed at Jannie's raised eyebrows and open mouth. "Ja, truly."

Jannie looked at his watch. "Let's get our bags and go." Sam's description of the ruined city of Plymouth he had seen on his way to London had filled Jannie with dread. He did not want to spend another restless night waking at every unusual sound, sweating and fearful.

Though there had been no further big air raids on London since the end of May, the Germans had not stopped attacking and their threat hung heavily over the country.

The doors of an official-looking car opened and out flew Ruth, closely followed by a laughing Sarah. Miriam got out more decorously.

"Oh my love, it is so good to be home," whispered Jannie, his face buried in Mimi's hair. She held him tightly, waiting for him to relax.

Henk lifted Ruth high above his head before twirling her around, then scooping up Sarah and kissing her. "Anyone would think you've been at sea for weeks," laughed Sarah, breathless when Henk finally put her down.

"It feels like it. Let's go home."

Sitting round Mimi's kitchen table, with Ruth perched upon Henk's knee, and jackets and ties slung over the backs of their chairs, Jannie and Henk took turns in telling her about their visit to Buckingham Palace.

"Like Christopher Robin?" Ruth asked, staring from one to the other.

"Almost," replied Henk, "Except we went to see the King."

"And then we saw our Queen," interjected Jannie.

"Who?" Miriam and Sarah spoke as one, scarcely believing what they had just heard.

"Queen Wilhelmina."

Henk reached into his jacket pocket, took out the small black leather box and put it on the table in front of Sarah. He gazed at her as she opened it and gasped. "What is it?" she whispered.

As Henk explained, Jannie said quietly. "He earned it, Sarah."

"What about you?" It was hard for Sarah to understand what Henk had done, for he had never told her about the time *De Ruyter* went to Dunkirk.

Jannie shrugged. "She also gave me a medal."

His frown stopped Henk from saying anything further. Jannie gave him a quick wink and moved the conversation on to Sam.

Chapter 40.

Cornwall

Soon after the harvest had been gathered, Sam reminded Mr Trevasso of his promise that he would be working with Ronnie Truscott on his traction engine.

"I haven't forgotten, Sam, but that's weeks away."

"I know, but can I help him get the engine ready?"

"Well," Mr T said seriously, "what about your work here?"

"I could go after evening milking." Sam had not realised Mr T was teasing him.

"I suppose so." Mr T sighed, "We'll just have to manage without you."

Once again Sam's hands and clothes were covered in oil, grease and coal dust as he and Ronnie prepared the big Fowler engine and threshing machine for the busy weeks ahead. Sometimes Annie rode over to watch them at work, a flask of cold tea and some sandwiches in a saddle bag. Once she stayed until they finished and then told Sam to get on Janet behind her. Only once, for it took her several washes to get the oily grime out of her clothes. She had not minded the extra work, but Sam was embarrassed.

Mr Truscott had seven farms on his list. Sam would join him when he went to Nanjigga Farm and stay on for the last two farms. "We don't usually take summer holidays, lad," Mr T told him one breakfast. "I suppose you've earned this one."

"Come on, Dad," Annie chipped in. "What about me?"

"You surely don't want to work on that stinking machine?" he replied.

"Oh Da-ad." The universal cry of children of all ages and nationalities made him laugh.

"Nay lass, though it would do you good."

Those summer breakfasts were light-hearted times, with the extended family teasing each other as they ate and talked until the nine o'clock news brought them back to earth with a bump. Sam was to look back on them as among the happiest days of his life.

Occasionally on calm evenings, Annie and Sam would launch the boat and drift along, trolling for bass or spinning for mackerel. Other times, Annie would borrow her father's shotgun at dusk and walk the fields with Sam and Aggie, hoping for a rabbit or two for the pot. They took it in turns with the gun, for Sam had as good an eye as Annie. Aggie was kept on her lead until she had a rabbit to "fetch."

Their working days were long, starting soon after sunrise and often going on until dusk. Young and old worked hard, slept deeply, with little time away from the farm and each other.

Sam was up and away before sunrise on 29th September, walking swiftly along the footpath to the barn where Ronnie kept his engine. The air was fresh and cool, the sky clear and the day full of promise.

A kettle was steaming on a brazier of glowing coals. While Ronnie was busy with his oil can, Sam made the tea and gave a shrill whistle.

"All set, boy?" Ronnie looked him up and down, glad to see he was wearing leather boots, cotton dungarees, a singlet under his jacket and an old cap. It was going to be a long, hot day.

"All set." Sam knew better than to talk too much. "I'll make breakfast."

"Aye." Ronnie tipped out the dregs, gave Sam his mug and went back to oiling and greasing.

It was not long before Ronnie hitched the big engine to the threshing machine, put their basket of victuals onboard and set off for Nanjigga Farm with Sam and his mate at his side.

Annie opened the farm gate to let them through, closed it behind them and squeezed onto the footplate as they made their way to the threshing ground.

"Where's the wind?" Ronnie asked her.

"It's very light," she replied, "From the south west."

She and Sam watched as Ronnie manoeuvred the threshing machine alongside the rick on the downwind side, with enough room for him to turn the engine so it was facing it.

Ronnie's mate walked over and got out the heavy canvas belt, placed it over the flywheel and dragged it onto the smaller wheel of the threshing machine. Ronnie checked its tension, looked around to make sure everyone was clear, and signalled Sam to engage the flywheel. He disengaged when Ronne gave him the thumbs up, stood back from the controls and looked around, surprised by how quickly the threshing ground had filled with people.

Once Mr T had them all in the right place, he nodded to Ronnie. Sam blew the whistle, engaged the flywheel – and threshing started.

It was a long day that none of them ever forgot, but not because of the heat, choking dust and noise, their aching muscles and the blessed relief when they stopped for a 'smoke-oh,' mugs of hot tea, flagons of cider, pasties, stories and laughter.

The sun was low in the sky when, above the clatter of the threshing machine, they heard the howl of aero engines, followed immediately by bullets hammering against the boiler, kicking up clouds of dust as they whanged and ricocheted off the engine. Sam looked up, saw the belly of an aircraft, knocked the engine out of gear and dived off the footplate, hearing another burst of gunfire as he went.

There was a moment of uncanny silence before someone started screaming.

Sam pushed himself off the ground, shaking his head to clear his mind before staring at the chaos around him, dread digging its icy hands into his belly.

"Annie! Annie!" Shouting with increasing desperation, he stumbled away from the engine.

The screaming stopped abruptly. People picked themselves off the ground, some standing as if stunned, others searching frantically for family or friends.

"Annie!" Sam was just about to shout again when she came staggering through the cloud of dust.

"Oh Sam, thank God. I saw you fall off the engine and thought you were dead." She flung her arms around him and burst into tears.

Instinctively, Sam put an arm around her, his free hand cradling her head upon his shoulder. Annie shuddered, sobbing and gasping for air, her tears carving lines through the soot and dirt on his chest.

Abruptly lifting her head, Annie stared about her. "Where's Mum?" Her voice rising, she screamed, "Where is my mother?"

Sam shook her, "Annie." He spoke sharply, recognising her rising panic. "Annie, stop."

She tried to pull away from him. "I have to find Mum." Trembling, tears flowing, Annie gazed helplessly round the yard. "She went to put the kettle on."

Sam sat Annie on the ground by a wheel of the engine when he saw Ronnie was on the footplate. "Stay here. I'll find her."

The dust, smoke and steam were clearing as Sam walked quickly towards the house.

"Oh no." He ran towards the shattered body lying on the grass. Falling to his knees, he felt Mrs T's neck, knowing she was dead, yet hoping, praying he would find a pulse. "Oh God," he whispered. "Oh my God."

He kissed her forehead without thinking before undoing her apron and spreading it over her unmarked face and the worst of her awful wounds.

Sam turned and ran back to find Mr Trevasso. One look at the boy's face, a glance at his bloodied hands and Mr T knew something dreadful had happened. He caught Sam as he slid to a halt, his gentle voice masking his anxiety.

"Who is it, lad? Who's been hurt?"

Sam took a deep breath before replying. "It's your wife, sir," his faint voice level as he broke the farmer's heart. "She's dead."

"No." Mr Trevasso staggered, took a pace back to steady himself and grasped the boy's hand. "Take me to her," he whispered.

Sam led him to his wife.

"Take Annie home, Sam. Don't let her see this." Before letting go of Sam's hand Mr T looked at it. "Clean yourself up first. Quickly mind."

Annie was sitting where he had left her, knees drawn up and head in her hands. Sam knelt beside her. "Let's go home, Annie." He took another breath. "Come on, Annie. Please."

Annie lifted her head to stare at Sam, her eyes red and breath uneven. Sam pulled her to her feet before she could say anything and hurried her away. "Come on," he urged her on, half running now. He stopped to knock on the kitchen door, fearful of what they might see inside.

"Oh Daddy." Annie fell forward. Mr T gathered her into his arms and carried her into the parlour, shielding her eyes from the body lying beneath a sheet on the kitchen table.

Sam walked slowly into the room, closing the door behind him. Going up to the table, he lifted the sheet away from Mrs T's head and stared at her beautiful face. He stretched out a hand to brush a curl of hair from her forehead and leant forward to kiss her again.

Mr Trevasso's muffled sob made Sam jump. He turned swiftly, started to speak and stopped; he had no words. Mr T came further into the room, partly closing the parlour door. "She's sleeping."

"Who?" Sam was confused.

"Annie, Sam." Mr T stood at the foot of the table and stared at the serene face of his beloved Martha. "She went to sleep before I could say anything." He shook his head. "She does not know you are dead, my love. How will I tell her?"

"Tell me what, Dad?" Annie stood in the open doorway, her mother hidden from view by Mr Trevasso.

"Nooooo...!" she cried as Mr T turned and she saw the body. Sam moved swiftly to her side. She pushed him away and took half a step forward.

"Noooo…" now the faintest of whispers, tears flooding down her cheeks. She clutched at her father, holding onto an arm with one hand as she went to pull the sheet away with the other.

"Don't." Gently, firmly, Sam lifted her hand clear and held onto it.

"Aye, lass." Her father's voice came as if from a great distance. "It's best not to." He pulled Annie towards him and wrapped his arms around her.

"Take her into the parlour, Mr T." Sam pushed him lightly. "Please."

Sam guided them to the sofa, fetched a rug and tucked it around them. "Stay here, sir. I'll get help."

Chapter 41.

"Oh God." Jannie put Sam's letter down. "Martha Trevasso's dead." He sighed, "Killed by a bloody German on his way home."

"How?" Miriam burst out.

"They shot at the threshing machine." Jannie scowled. "On their way back from a bombing raid." He stood, anger coursing through him. "Christ almighty, they're a heartless bunch of bastards."

Handing the letter to Miriam, Jannie said, "I'm going to see the colonel."

Lady Teagle also had a letter from Sam. She read it twice before telephoning Colonel Blackhurst. As requested, he made a call to Plymouth, bringing forward the collection of certain information and arranging a date for its return.

Thus it was that Jannie and Miriam had a swift journey by car to Plymouth and a very much slower one to Penzance where they were met and delivered to the farm by Jim Semmens.

'Sad business," Jim said, opening Miriam's door. "I'll see you tomorrow."

The chapel was packed and the service sombre. Flowers picked in hedgerows and fields gradually covered Martha's grave as her many friends filed slowly past. Frank remained stony-faced throughout the ordeal. Annie wept quietly as the eulogy was delivered by the minister. Leaning against her father, she held on to Sam's hand when he passed her his clean handkerchief, drawing strength from both men. It took all Sam's self-control not to cry.

"Take Annie home, Sam." Recognising that Annie was stretched to breaking point, Mr Trevasso steered her gently out of the graveyard and away from the gaze of the many mourners who were beginning to walk up to the hotel. Sam put his hand on Annie's elbow and whispered, "We had better let Aggie out."

That was enough to get a faint nod. She slipped her hand into his as they walked away and did not let go until they reached the farm and Sam had to open the gate.

Aggie was, of course, delighted to see them, dancing around their feet and jumping up into one or the other's arms. She was impossible to ignore and they could not bring themselves to keep her out of the kitchen. "Right," Sam gazed at Annie, "let's get changed and take Aggie for a walk."

Sam had forgotten to shut the kitchen door so Aggie scampered upstairs and onto Annie's bed, tail wagging, tongue lolling, her eyes inviting Annie to sit beside her, to put her feet up and put her arms around her, which, of course, Annie did. Aggie's warmth and the comfort of her unconditional love released more tears in a sudden wave of loss and yearning.

Aggie lifted her head when Sam tapped on the door. Puzzled by the silence, he lifted the latch and pulled it open. The sight of Annie sleeping on her side, the strain of the past week smoothed from her face, her mouth slightly open and the dog cradled in her arms, formed a picture that lived with him all his life. His sudden breathlessness and the unexpected butterflies in his stomach brought a new and strange weakness to his limbs.

As it was obvious Annie needed to sleep and Aggie showed no inclination to move, Sam backed out, half closed the door and swiftly changed into his work clothes. There were cows to be brought in, milking to be started and all the other demands of the farm to be met.

Frank did not stay long at the wake. He slipped quietly out of a side door, stood for a moment to get his emotions under control and began walking home. Jannie, Miriam and Betty Hartley hurried after him. "May we walk with you?" Jannie asked.

"Of course." Frank was relieved to have company; the new emptiness of his life was almost unbearable.

"I'll give you a hand with the milking," Betty said after a while.

"Thank you," Frank looked at her. "Best change, m'dear, you don't want to spoil those shoes."

"We'll help," Mimi looked for and received Jannie's nod. "If you show us what to do."

Greatly relieved, Frank stood a little taller.

"Won't be long." Betty and her two guests hurried to the Count House. Frank continued down the hill, walking a little more purposefully.

Surprised to find Sam alone in the milking parlour, Frank hurried over. "Where's Annie?" Frowning, his voice harsh, he growled, "I thought you were looking after her."

Sam looked up without pausing the steady jetting of milk into the pail, "She's asleep, Mr T. Worn out, poor girl." A sudden, impish grin lit up his face. "Aggie's looking after her."

"What?" Mr T looked startled. "Where?"

"Don't be cross, sir." Sam looked at his boss. "They're in Annie's room."

Mr Trevasso blew out his cheeks. "Why should I be cross?" He pushed his fingers through his hair. "It doesn't matter. Nothing matters any…"

"Don't say that." Sam stood. He shook Mr T's arm. "Everything matters. Now more than ever." He gazed at Annie's grieving father. "We must do our duty." He shook Frank again. "It is all we can do."

Chapter 42.

"Like this, Jannie," said Sam, squeezing the cow's teat before tugging it gently and directing the jet of milk into a pail. Jannie smiled fondly at the back of Sam's head, masking his amusement when Sam turned round. Changing places, Jannie tucked his head into the warm, sweet-smelling flank of Sam's favourite cow, gently took a teat in each hand, squeezed, tugged and failed to produce a drop. He tried again with equal lack of success before admitting defeat and leaving Betty and Sam to milk the herd. Feeding the hens, geese and pigs was simple and satisfying.

Once finished, he went back to the milking parlour to ask Sam where Frank was. He was not surprised to find him leaning against the same gate where they had spoken all those months ago.

"Cigarette?"

Frank sighed, turned to Jannie and took one, his hand shaking slightly. They smoked in silence until Frank pinched the end of his fag and pulled out his pipe. "Sam gave me quite a bollocking," he said as he filled it. "Told me we had to do our duty."

"That's what he said to me," wonder in Jannie's voice, "after we'd buried Henri and Dirk."

Frank pushed himself away from the gate to light his pipe. Once it was drawing satisfactorily, he turned to Jannie. "He has a wise head on those young shoulders of his."

"Ja, Frank, war does that." He spat out a leaf of tobacco. "Sam has been through so much." He looked at Frank, "What is it doing to him?"

"Much as it did to you, Jannie." Sorrow was etched deep into Frank's weary face. "And in a very small way, to me. I never thought it would come here."

"You were in the last lot?" Jannie was incredulous. "I didn't think farmers were called up."

A brief smile flickered. "I wasn't. I volunteered when I was eighteen and drove horses in France for the last few months of the War." He tapped his pipe on the gate. "My older brother ran the farm." His voice dropped. "Until the 'flu took him."

"*Stront*." He put his hand on Frank's. "What will you do now?"

"I will do my duty!" Frank cleared his throat. "Keep going." He wiped away a tear. "What else can I do?" Angry at his weakness, he looked at Jannie. "Annie needs me."

"So does Sam," Jannie reminded him.

"We need each other," Frank looked pensive, "and so does Annie. She's very close to him."

"Does that worry you?" Jannie and Miriam had their concerns.

"No." His expression softened. "He is kind. We need kindness."

Gazing across his farm, he whispered, "And he learns quickly. He will look after Annie and look after this land."

"If you ever need more help, Frank, you can always call on Miriam and me." Jannie shrugged. "Neither of us knows anything about farming but we're not too old to learn."

"Thank you." Frank was deeply moved by Jannie's offer. "I won't forget."

They were interrupted by the excited barking of Aggie as she raced towards them, Annie and Sam some distance behind her.

Jannie put his hand on Frank's shoulder. "Keep talking to Martha." Frank closed his eyes to hide the pain as Jannie went on, "I talk to Henri every day. Tell him everything."

"Oh Dad." Annie flung herself into Frank's arms. "I missed milking."

"Never mind, my love, Miss Hartley helped us."

"Jannie didn't," Sam laughed, "but he did feed the pigs."

"And hens; geese too." Jannie joined in. "Sam's not a very good teacher."

"Nee, baas, you're too old to learn."

Frank looked at Jannie and laughed as they walked slowly back to the farm, keeping the conversation light until they came to the ruined threshing machine.

"I'll be glad to see the back of this," Frank muttered as they hurried past.

Betty, Jannie and Miriam left soon after supper, hurrying up the hill to get back before it was fully dark; a thin sliver of the nearly new moon hung bright above the western horizon.

Jannie lit the sitting room fire while Betty made a pot of tea and Miriam drew the blackout curtains.

"That poor man, he looks so lost." Mimi put her cup down. "How is he going to cope?"

Jannie gave a brief laugh. "Sam told him to do his duty."

"What?" Betty looked shocked.

"You have to do your duty, that's what he said." Jannie looked at her. "It's a lesson he learned from Henri." He smiled. "He said the same to me."

"Well," interjected Mimi, "it's how he lives his life. And that's how Frank will cope in the days and months to come."

Chapter 43.

"How is Sam?" Jannie repeated Henk's question as they settled by the fire Sarah had lit in their sitting room. "Changed," he nodded. "He's very mature for his age. Mature and wise."

"Yes," Mimi added, "but still a boy at heart." She laughed. "Especially at heart. He is oblivious to the fact that Annie is obviously in love with him."

"Really" Sarah found that hard to believe.

"Yes, my dear, really. He's very protective of her, but doesn't notice her reaction."

"Hmm." Sarah chuckled. "There'll be fireworks when he does."

The death of Mrs Trevasso changed Sam in another way. It fanned the spark of hatred that had been smouldering in his mind since Henri was killed, turning it into a fire that, at times, threatened to overwhelm him. Annie was the first to notice this, sensing a new hardness, a coldness in Sam's reactions when listening to the news. Mr T heard it in his voice whenever they talked about what they had heard.

***

"Sam," Annie sounded anxious, "we must get the boat further up." It was nearly dark, high tide was in an hour, the wind was already strong and a full gale was forecast. They should have done this earlier in the day. However, the labourer Mr T hired to help while he was away in Truro had not turned up, leaving them with much to do.

It started raining as they rigged the tackle; heavy, cold, stinging drops driven ashore by the half gale, cooling them while they sweated on the windlass as the boat inched above the high-water mark. It was a foul, black night. Chilled and half-blinded by the rain and spray, Sam yelled to Annie, "All secure. Let's get home."

Annie's words were lost in the thunder of waves crashing ashore. Sam reached for her hand when a sudden gust blew her off-balance.

"This way." She pulled him up the slope and into the lee of a hedge.

Both were soaked and shivering; it was no place to linger. Annie hesitated, trying to picture the way home. *Up the track to the gate, then downhill across the field, about two hundred yards, roughly north west.* They should get home safely, as long as the gale kept blowing from the south west.

"Thank you, God," Annie whispered as she slammed the door. Sam splashed his way cautiously to the stove, dried his hands on a tea towel and reached for the shelf where the matches lived. He was shivering so violently it took two matches before he lit the lamp. Annie hurried to the stove, crouched down and opened the doors to let the heat out.

Sam opened the damper to increase the draft, slid the kettle onto the hottest plate and made a pot of tea. "Here, drink this." Annie wrapped her hands round the mug, glad to feel warmth slowly returning.

They sat on the floor, backs to the stove, sipping their tea, soaked and still shivering.

"This will never do!" Sam jumped to his feet, ran upstairs and returned with two large towels and a hot water bottle.

"Here." He took Annie's empty mug from her hands. "Get out of those clothes before you catch your death of cold." Handing her the towels, he added, "I'll put the hot water bottle in your bed."

Annie was bending over the stove when he came back, still shivering, one towel over her head and shoulders, the other wrapped around her body. Without a second thought, Sam put his hands on her shoulders and began to rub vigorously.

At Annie's muffled protest, he said, a little too quickly, "This is what we do in Holland. When you fall through the ice."

She relaxed a little as he continued rubbing, but tensed again when he started to rub her back. Sam took a kitchen towel from the dresser, knelt beside her and began rubbing her left leg.

"Stop." Annie's voice was gentle. "I can do that." She looked at Sam. "Go and get some more towels." When he hesitated, she snapped. "Hurry. You're freezing."

Sam scurried away. Too cold to think clearly, he was soon back, towels in his hands.

Annie laughed as alarm flashed across his face when he realised he would have to take his clothes off in front of her. It did not feel the same as changing on the beach.

"Come on silly." Annie pushed him towards the stove, "I won't look."

Once dry, Sam piled their wet clothes into a bucket while Annie put a pan of soup on the hob.

"That's better. Thanks." Sam wiped his bowl clean, tossed the crust to Aggie and got up, one hand gripping the towel round his waist. "Get to bed. I'll tidy up."

"Don't bother with the dishes. We can do them in the morning."

Sam grinned at her, "I don't mind. And it's warm in here."

With the kitchen tidy, the stove topped up and damper closed, Sam shooed Aggie through the front door to do her business in the lee of the house. It was still blowing hard, rain swirling past in the dim glow from the open door. Aggie hurried in, shook herself vigorously and looked at Sam.

Closing the door on the night, Sam dried his puppy, gave her a biscuit and lit a candle before turning the wick down on the kitchen lamp. Boy and dog went upstairs. Sam tapped on Annie's door before opening it. Aggie ran in and jumped onto her bed. Sam closed her door, hurried to his room, swiftly put on his pyjamas, blew out the candle and buried himself under his bedclothes.

He was fast asleep when Annie crept into his room and slid under the bedclothes. He did not stir when she put her head on his pillow, an arm over his back and a leg over his. Annie felt her heart thumping, loud enough to wake the dead. She closed her eyes, warm, comforted, safe.

Sam woke with a start; he tried to stir and could not move. Sitting up, he flung the bedclothes to one side.

Annie giggled.

"Wha'?" Still half-asleep, Sam patted the body beside him. "Who's that?"

"It's me, silly." Annie giggled again. "Who d'you think it was?" She pushed his chest. "Lie down and go back to sleep."

Sam did as he was told, pulling the bedclothes over them as he turned to face her.

"What are you doing here?" he whispered.

"Getting warm."

"Oh." Thoroughly confused, Sam lay on his back, his hands behind his head

"That's better," Annie whispered as she snuggled against him, her head upon his chest. Sam put an arm around her and whispered, "Night, night."

It was Aggie, scratching and whining at the door, that woke Sam. Annie was leaning on one arm, gazing at him in the grey light of the early morning. "Sleep well?" she asked, her eyes dancing with mischief.

Sam stared at her, wonder and joy in his heart. He reached up to put a tentative hand on her cheek, a shy smile twitching his lips. "Oh yes." He frowned. "You should let Aggie in."

Annie raced the dog to the bed, jumped in and laughed. "Now go back to sleep." They had another hour before it was time to get up and sleep was precious, though not as precious as their nascent emotions as they lay chastely in each other's arms.

Chapter 44.

Their second Christmas in Hampshire was even more joyful than the first for the two families, and the twenty children who now attended their school. Ruth made a beautiful angel in the Nativity play, Jannie and Henk again attended Midnight Mass – and Sarah told Miriam she was pregnant.

"Oh my dear girl," said Miriam, promptly bursting into tears. Dumbfounded, Sarah stared helplessly while Mimi searched her pockets for a handkerchief before wiping her eyes, blowing her nose and laughing. "Well," said Mimi eventually, 'that is the best news I've heard all year." She blew her nose again. "I don't know why I'm crying when I am so happy." She held out her hands to Sarah. "How long have you known?"

Sarah took her hands and hugged her, relieved, confused and delighted in equal measures. "Three months," Sarah said. "we didn't want to tell anyone until we were certain." She smiled fondly as she remembered Henk's reaction, his huge bellow of delight and how careful they had to be not to let Ruth hear them talking about the baby. "It was a big secret to keep in a small place."

It was the very best news at the end a terrible year, with the death of Martha still weighing heavily on them.

Japan's attack on Pearl Harbour, followed by Hitler's declaration of war on America, prompted a flicker of hope. This was brutally extinguished by the loss of *HMS Renown* and *Prince of Wales*, and the speed with which Japan's victorious armies swept through South East Asia and the Western Pacific islands.

A few days before Sam's birthday, Sam and Annie walked up to their favourite place, a sheltered hollow in the top field. Ever since Martha's death they had gone there whenever they wanted to be alone.

"I'm eighteen soon," Sam started.

"No you're not." There were no longer any secrets between these two.

"I'm not," agreed Sam, "But my passport says I am. And," puffing out his chest, "I look eighteen."

Annie could not disagree, not since Sam's voice had broken and he had started shaving

He gazed at Annie, fearful of her reaction to what he had to say.

She gave a fleeting smile. "Come on, Sam. Spit it out."

"I'm joining the Navy."

His words fell like heavy blows, driving the air from her lungs.

Annie gasped and clutched his hands. "Why?" She was crying now. "Why, Sam?"

"To kill Germans." Sam's face was like granite, his eyes cold and voice harsh. "I swore an oath on your mother's coffin."

"When?"

He wished she would not look at him so pitifully and closed his eyes, thinking, *God, I love you.*

"What did you say?"

Sam did not realise he had spoken aloud. He stroked her hands. "I love you, Annie," smiling, "I have loved you ever since you pushed me overboard."

Annie blushed at the memory. She had never forgotten the day she stripped off and swam out to the boat, thinking Sam was in trouble. Nor had she forgotten the way he looked at her.

"Jesus, Sam.' Annie shook her head. "You tell me you're going away and then say you love me."

She pulled her hands free and ran off.

Sam walked slowly back to the farm, dreading Mr Trevasso's reaction.

He need not have worried. Seeing Annie's tear-streaked face, her father sat her on his knee, just as he always had done when she was little, and listened while she poured her heart out. Desperately wishing Martha was here, Frank listened without interrupting, save the one time he took a handkerchief from his pocket and passed it to her with a quiet, "Here, blow your nose."

Annie wiped her eyes, blew her nose and finished telling him about Sam without crying again.

He kissed the top of her head before leaning back to look at her and ask, "Do you love him?"

"Oh Dad, of course I do." She stared at her father. "Didn't you guess?"

Frank smiled, "Well," he teased, "I did wonder." Sensing tears were not far away, he hurried on, "But not for long. When did you know?"

Annie half closed her eyes, gave a little sigh and whispered, "When he first arrived." She sat a little straighter in her father's arms, "But I only realised that later. When I saw him…" Her voice tailed off.

"When you saw him what?" Frank stared at her. "Why've you gone red?" His voice had sharpened.

"Oh Dad, nothing bad." Annie smiled to herself and told him how Sam had tricked her into believing he was drifting out to sea and how she was so worried she stripped off without thinking and how angry she'd been with him, so angry she'd started punching him and how he had to hold her to make her stop. She took a breath, looked deep into her father's eyes, saw the smile hiding there and whispered "It was when I saw how he looked at me." She shook her head slightly. "He'd never looked at me like that before."

"Like what?" Frank was intrigued.

"It was as if he'd suddenly found something special and didn't know what to do with it. I wanted to kiss him. I nearly did." She gave a little laugh. "I don't know what he saw in my face, but he let me go. So I pushed him overboard."

Frank laughed. "Probably just as well."

"It probably was." Annie slipped off her father's knee. "I'll put the kettle on, he'll be here soon."

Picking up his pipe, Frank pointed the stem at Annie. "Your mother and I hoped he'd stay here, marry you and take on the farm."

"So did he, Dad, but he put his hand on Mum's coffin and swore he would kill Germans. You heard him. He has to do that first, then he will come home and marry me."

"Killing Germans won't bring her back, my dear."

"I know, I know. But he swore an oath."

Chapter 45.

Sam wrote to Lady Teagle in April, asking her how to join the Navy and making this point; "I must be a gunner, milady. If the Navy tells me to be an engineer, I will join the Army." Dropping the letter onto her lap, Emma folded her hands together and lowered her head in prayer. "God help you, Sam," she breathed, "I wish you had not asked me."

She went to her desk and wrote a short note to William.

While Sam could easily have walked into the Naval Recruiting Office in Penzance, as his letter to Lady Teagle showed, he was worried he might be compelled to train as an engineer.

Admiral Teagle did what was necessary. Sam received a letter from the Admiralty a week before his 'eighteenth' birthday thanking him for volunteering and telling him where to report for his medical.

Thinking Sam looked younger than his stated age, the doctor scrutinised his passport with extra care. The forgery was good and Sam was undoubtedly healthy. He was told he would be sent his travel warrant together with a letter confirming he was fit for service at sea and telling him where and when to report.

"Thank you, sir." As Sam bowed and left the examination, the doctor shook his head. "That boy is never eighteen." He shrugged and turned to the next in the queue.

Sam walked up Market Jew Street confused by the conflicting emotions he was feeling. Elation was tempered by anxiety, relief by the sense of impending loss. Above all, his love for Annie tore at the certainty of his decision.

Home again and in his work clothes, he found Annie and Mr Trevasso leading the horses back to the stable. Annie handed the reins to her father and ran to Sam.

"Well?" She took hold of his arm. "What happened?"

Sam hung his head, unable to meet her eyes. "They accepted me."

Annie gave a low moan. "Oh Sam." Tears filled her eyes. "When…" She was unable to finish.

"I don't know." He looked up, desperate to comfort her, knowing there was no comfort he could give. "A few days."

Annie closed her eyes, took a deep breath and put her arms round him. Heedless of her father, she whispered, "Well then, we mustn't waste a minute," kissed him lightly on the cheek and stood back. "Come and help us in the stable."

Sensing what Annie was doing, Mr Trevasso played his part, hurrying the big horses into their stable before asking Sam to help them with the harnesses, their feed and water. Sam threw himself into the work, his mood rapidly lightening.

"Right lad, time for a cuppa before milking. Put the kettle on." He nodded to Annie. "Give him a hand. There's cake in the tin."

If she had looked back, Annie would have seen sorrow chasing anxiety across her father's face. Frank was desperately worried about Sam. "Shit," he muttered, shaking his head, "you're too young for this." He went about his work mechanically, talking to Martha, as he had ever since she had been killed. Jannie was right. It helped to ease the pain.

Annie kicked the kitchen door shut as Sam took her into his arms and hugged her so hard that she gasped. Letting her go, he put his hands onto her cheeks, his eyes never leaving hers. It was the first, electric, unforgettable time they kissed.

Tea had become a social time once the harvest was in. The table was now covered with a clean table cloth and laid with care. "It's what Mum wanted," Annie told her father the first time she and Sam had changed what used to be a brief pause in their working day into a moment they came to cherish, a moment when they shared memories, dreams and problems.

Mr T looked at Annie and then Sam. They looked flustered. "What's happened?"

"What d'you mean?" Annie looked anywhere but at her father

"You look different."

Blushing but determined, Sam bowed to Mr Trevasso. "Sir, please, I would like to marry Annie?"

Frank blinked and looked at his daughter. He had not expected this. "D'you want to marry Sam? You're both very young."

Surprised, delighted and scared, Annie stared at Sam who smiled at her. "You haven't answered."

She smiled back. "You haven't asked me."

"But we kissed." Confused, Sam stuttered, "I thought that meant…"

Annie smiled. "Of course I will. If Dad says yes.'

Frank laughed. "I don't have any choice, do I? Not now you've kissed each other." He closed his eyes, wishing Martha was here, hoping he had not made a mistake, amazed at the boy's innocence, wondering if he ought to tell Sam about the facts of life.

Chapter 46.

Annie thought the best birthday present Sam received was the letter from the Admiralty, telling him to report to *HMS Raleigh* in Saltash on Thursday 28th May. She had feared he would have to leave that same day, not ten days later.

Equally relieved, Mr T made another appointment to see his solicitor in Truro, determined he would not be away when Sam departed. He was going to change his will.

A few cards were propped against the milk jug when Sam came in. He grinned at Mr Trevasso, "Sorry to keep you waiting," washed his hands and sat down next to Annie.

"Aren't you going to open them?" Annie loved birthdays.

All the cards were from Hampshire, as Lady Teagle had returned to their house in Droxford when Admiral Teagle went back to sea. Annie poured the tea while Sam was opening, reading and passing the cards to Frank. "Golly," Sam looked up, "Sarah's having her baby next month. Henk is making a cradle for it."

"Lucky Sarah."

Frank glanced quickly at his daughter before looking away. She had never expressed any interest in babies before; his conversation with Sam had just become rather important.

"Time for presents." Frank fetched them from the parlour while Sam cleared the table. He watched carefully as Annie put a small package in front of the boy, willing her to be strong. Sam untied the ribbon, lifted the small, leather box from the wrapping paper and held it in his hand. He looked at the girl, saw she was trembling, took her hand and asked gently, "What is it?"

"Open it and see." Annie sat down abruptly and eyed Sam anxiously as he pressed the button on the side. He gasped when the lid popped open and looked first at Frank and then at Annie. "I can't take this."

Frank put his hand on Sam's when he started to push the box towards him. "Please, Sam. Listen." He turned to Annie. "You tell him."

Annie put one hand on Sam's and the other on her father's. "We want you to have it." Her eyes big and tears not far away. "It's Mum's."

Sam whispered, "I know."

Annie raised the heavy gold wedding ring slightly before pulling it clear by the cord that passed through it.

"Wear this close to your heart, my Sam, until you put it on my finger." She leant forward, put the cord over Sam's head and whispered, "Now we are engaged."

Frank retrieved his hand to wipe away a tear before clapping his hands.

"And now you must kiss your fiancée."

After a moment of joyful shy confusion, Frank nudged Sam. "Put her down now, boy, and get three glasses."

He lifted a bottle of champagne from the sink, removed its cork with a satisfying 'pffft' and poured carefully. Clinking his glass against Annie's and then Sam's, he toasted "My beloved Martha," his voice husky.

"Martha," whispered Sam while Annie murmured, "Mum."

Frank was touched to see the young people close their eyes.

He paused for a moment before declaring, his voice firm, "To my darling daughter and to Sam. Congratulations"

He beamed at them. "One more toast. Happy Birthday Sam and welcome to the family."

With that, Frank sat down, picked up a rectangular parcel and handed it to Sam.

'What's this?" Sam held up one of the keys to the farmhouse.

"It's yours, Sam." Frank smiled at the boy. "The key to your home."

"I don't understand." Sam looked from Annie to Frank. "Why have you given it to me?"

Suddenly serious, Frank told him: "I'm transferring the farm to you and Annie as soon as you get married. I'll be here to help, but you two will be running it."

Flabbergasted, Sam turned to Annie, "Did you know he was doing this?"

"Not till yesterday."

Sam shook himself. "I don't know anything about farms."

"Not much, lad, but you're a quick learner." Frank grinned at him, "You don't mind taking orders from a woman, do you?"

"Of course not." Sam had been bossed about by his mother all his life. "Why?"

"Well, Annie's the farmer. You'll be helping her."

"That's a relief." Sam laughed and went round to shake Frank's hand. "Thank you, sir."

"Less of the sir, Sam." Frank got up and put his arms around him and Annie. "Bless you, my dears. You've made this old man very happy." He laughed. "Let's get the cows in."

Sam opened the rest of his presents after supper, putting on the wristwatch from Tante Mimi before settling down at the table to study Jannie's book of paintings and drawings of life onboard *De Ruyter*. Frank and Annie sat either side of him as he explained what was going on in each picture, learning more about Sam and his life in Holland than he had ever told them before.

"You'll have to read this," Sam told Frank, as he picked up the book that Sir William and Lady Teagle had given him. "It's about Dunkirk."

Sam had not seen the inscription on the flyleaf of *The Nine Days Wonder*.

To Sam, with grateful thanks for your service onboard De Ruyter signed *William Teagle, C-in-C Nore* above another signature, *John Masefield*.

Having pointed it out, Frank yawned and announced: "I'm off to bed. Don't be late you two." He kissed Annie, patted Sam on the shoulder and went upstairs, happier than he had been ever since Martha was killed.

Chapter 47.

Jannie pushed the letter from Sam across the table to Miriam without a word. She read it, sighed and leant back in her chair, sorrow mixing with anxiety. "Why?"

She flicked the letter away from her. "What's he done that for?"

"He told me he swore an oath." Jannie picked up the letter and shook it. "To kill Germans."

"For goodness sake." Miriam looked at Jannie. "I suppose he said it was his duty?"

"He did, my love. It's all he knows." He reached for her hand. "That's all any of us know."

"He was doing his duty," she said with asperity. "Farming is a reserved occupation."

"It is, my love, but Sam has volunteered and been accepted. There's nothing we can do about that."

"Hmm." Miriam cocked her head to look at Jannie. "We could always tell the Navy how old he really is."

"No we couldn't." Jannie was shocked by her suggestion. "He'd never trust us again."

"I know, but he wouldn't be going to sea."

"Please forget it, my love." Jannie passed her a cigarette, lit it and took one for himself. "Sam's sense of duty is all he has."

"What about Annie?"

"I know, I know. The poor girl will be heartbroken. So will he." He took a deep drag at his cigarette, not daring to say 'it is the War.'

Reading his mind, Miriam smiled at her dear, troubled man. "I'm glad you didn't say: it is the War."

Jannie ruffled her hair and sat down. What he told her came as a great surprise.

"Listen, my love, I told Frank we'd come and help him if he asked us."

"What?" Miriam was flummoxed. "Why didn't you tell me?"

"I forgot." Shamefaced, Jannie gazed helplessly at her. "There was so much going on, so much grief." He gave a crooked smile. "You know what it was like."

"I do." She looked at him. "What did he say?"

'Thank you. That's all." Jannie paused, "And I won't forget." He laughed. "Which is unlike me."

"You'd better tell Henk, and let the colonel know."

"I suppose so. Though I don't expect Frank will want us."

Frank did all he could to give Annie and Sam as much time together as work allowed, thankful the Ministry had granted his request for two lasses from the Women's Land Army to help him. Jenny and Kate were cheerful, competent young women, happy with their billets in the town. They settled quickly into the routine of Nanjigga Farm, much to Frank's relief.

Sam, reserved and conscious of the days slipping by, remained an enigma to the girls, while Annie, although equally aware of how little time she had left, made a determined effort to make them welcome.

"I'm off to Truro tomorrow," Frank told Annie two days before Sam departed. "I've an afternoon meeting so I'll stay the night."

"Thanks Dad."

He grinned.

"I was young once."

Sam banged on Annie's door early on his last morning, calling, "Coming for a walk?" as he opened it to let Aggie out. He was determined to remain cheerful and not let Annie see how scared he was. Frank knew what Sam would be feeling. No-one who had seen active service could fail to recognise Sam's forced good humour.

Frank handed them each a mug of tea as they came into the kitchen. "Here, drink this before you put your boots on. Breakfast will be on the table in an hour."

He watched as they ran across the yard before sitting at the table for his first pipe of the day, thankful that Annie had readily agreed not to come to the station with them.

Farewells were best done in private.

"All set?" Frank's voice was gentle. Sam nodded, his eyes wide open as he gazed around the room. "What have you done with your valuables?" Frank insisted that Sam leave them behind, knowing how light-fingered some new recruits would be.

"They're in my kitbag. Annie's looking after them." He looked at Frank, "All except my watch and writing case. Just like you said."

"What about the ring?"

"I put it round her neck." Sam blinked a couple of times. He steadied himself. "I'll go and say goodbye to her now."

"It's only twelve weeks, Sam." Frank gave a brief smile. "They'll soon be over." Sam jumped when the guard blew his whistle. Frank held out his hand, "Remember what you told me?"

"One hand for the ship…"

"…and one for yourself," they said together and shook hands.

"God, Jim, that took me back." Frank's hands were trembling as he lit his pipe. "He's too bloody young to go to war."

"He's been there already," Jim reminded him.

"Yes," Frank gave a huge sigh. "Yes he has. He's only going this time because Martha was killed."

Jim glanced at him. "I didn't know that. I am sorry Frank."

"So am I. But nothing I said made any difference." He drew a deep lungful of smoke. "He swore an oath." Exhaling and waving the smoke away, he added, "He really hates the Germans." He paused. "They got bombed and shot up at Dunkirk. You knew that, didn't you?"

"Aye." Jim concentrated on his driving.

"His captain and one of the Dutch crew were killed, along with several soldiers."

"I heard about that."

"And his family should have escaped, but couldn't." Frank closed his eyes for a moment. "What's all that done to the boy?"

'Nothing good," Jim replied. "It is a very great shame about Martha. She was a good woman." He slowed as he spoke, choosing his words carefully. "I do not believe she would want the boy to be going to war on account of her being killed."

Frank sighed. "She would not." He looked out of the window as they drove down the road to his farm and said, half to himself, "I do hope Annie will manage while he's away."

As Jim stopped the car, he looked at his friend with great compassion. "She will surprise you, Frank. You mark my words. She is a fine young woman."

Annie did indeed surprise Frank, but not until Sam had sailed in *HMS Persephone*.

Sam had ample time to consider the consequences of his actions during his long, lonely train journey to Plymouth.

The shock of sudden, loud orders, endless marching, the obsessive cleanliness demanded by instructors, was much as Lady Teagle described. So too was his confusion as he struggled to make sense of the orders and the disorientation he felt until he found his feet. It was small comfort to know that every new recruit was feeling the same.

Gradually, Sam began to enjoy himself, revelling in the sense of comradeship fostered on the parade ground, in the gym and on the water. Pride in appearance, in the cleanliness of their quarters and efficiency in executing orders came naturally to him. By the end of his six weeks' training, Samuel da Souza was recognised as an exceptionally talented young man and transferred with a glowing report to The Cambridge Gunnery School at Wembury.

It did not take the gunnery instructors long to recognise that Sam was a naturally good shot with both rifle and Lewis gun. He enjoyed the rhythm and balance required of a 4-inch gun crew to keep firing until

Cease Fire was ordered, and found the four and eight barrelled 2-pounder pom-poms noisy and exhilarating.

It was only when he was strapped behind a 20 mm Oerlikon gun and taught how to aim and fire at a target towed behind an aircraft, that his instructors discovered just how good a shot he was. He passed out as a Seaman Gunner (Anti-Aircraft) Second Class, proudly sewing his badge onto his uniform before the final parade.

Once again able to have a lift in a naval car, Jannie and Miriam arrived in Plymouth a day later for a brief and somewhat unsatisfactory visit. Sam was on duty in the barracks until 1600 on each of their two afternoons together and had to be back by 2200. Tea, followed by a walk on Plymouth Hoe and an evening meal in their hotel, passed swiftly as they chatted their way through the little time they had.

Sam wanted to know all about Sarah's baby, Henri Dirk, and how Ruth was getting on and what Henk was like as a father. Jannie learnt all about the intricacies of Swedish Oerlikon guns, naval training and why bell-bottom trousers had seven horizontal creases in them. Sam told Miriam a great deal more about Annie than he realised, to her delight. She and Jannie had to steer his conversation to Frank before he told them how Mr Trevasso had given him his own key to the farm and that he and Annie would be taking it over after the War.

They were delighted when Sam told them he had been granted ten days' pre-deployment leave before he joined the light cruiser *HMS Persephone* in Devonport Dockyard, reporting at 0800 on Monday 10th August 1942.

"Well," said Jannie at the end of their last evening together, "Don't forget to write." He smiled at the boy, "And remember, never volunteer."

"Thanks, Jannie. For everything." Sam held out his hand.

Jannie pulled Sam to him, said quietly, "We'll be thinking of you," and stood back.

Miriam put her hands on Sam's shoulders and gazed at him for a moment before closing her eyes to pray, "May it be Your will that You will lead us in peace ..." She sensed Sam stiffen before he joined her in saying; "and cause us to reach our destination in life, joy and peace. Save us from every enemy and ambush …" Sam wept quietly as she continued, only joining in again as she said, "May You confer Your blessings upon the work of our hands and grant us grace, kindness and mercy in Your eyes."

"Thank you, Tante Mimi. That is what my father prayed when I left to join *De Ruyter*." Miriam hugged Sam, then kissed him on the forehead. "May God bless you, my dear."

He held onto her for a moment, whispered, "I love you," and walked swiftly away.

Chapter 48.

Annie ran towards the carriage as Sam tipped his hat to the left, straightened his uniform and stepped onto the platform at Penzance. Flinging her arms around him, laughing and crying with joy, she gasped as he picked her up and swung her round before gently putting her down to look at her.

They both started to speak at once, stopped and laughed. "You first." Annie, surprised at how much more confident Sam sounded, leant forward and kissed him. "Hello Sam," she whispered, shy and a little uncertain. "You look well."

Sam took both her hands in his. "Hello Annie." He gazed at her. "Let's go home."

Jim adjusted the mirror so they would not feel spied on in the back of his taxi. He wondered how long it would be before Sam put his arm round Annie, smiling to himself when he rightly guessed it would be before they had left Penzance.

He slowed as they reached the mine stack near the quarry. "Like me to stop, Sam?"

"Please."

Sam jumped out, closed his eyes and breathed in the warm, honeyed scent of summer. Laughing, he told Annie, "This is where Jim stopped when we'd just arrived. To look at the sea. I never knew it could be so blue." He turned to Jim. "Our North Sea is green," adding, "this is a very special place, isn't it?"

"Aye lad, but we'd best not dawdle. Mr T is waiting for you."

Frank heard the car coming down the hill and was standing by the open gate with Aggie at his feet when they arrived.

Sam caught his dog when she leapt up to greet him, wriggling with joy and licking his face as he tried to speak.

It was a joyous home-coming.

By the time Aggie calmed down, they were in the kitchen and the front of Sam's uniform was covered with dog hairs. "I'm glad it wasn't wet," was all he said as he put her down. Frank and Annie watched, amazed at the contortions required to get out of his tight-fitting jumper, until his muffled voice asked for help.

"That's better." He looked at their faces and laughed as he tried to smooth his tousled hair. "It's only our best uniform that is so tight.

"Why?"

"Oh," replied Sam with the airy confidence of an ancient mariner, "that's so they don't get caught on anything or blown over our heads when we go aloft."

Annie was intrigued, but saved her questions for later. She had made Sam a cake for tea.

There was much to talk about in between cups of tea and slices of cake.

Frank was impressed by the subtle changes in Sam, evident in his posture, the way he held his head, the steadiness of his eyes, even the tone of his voice. Thankfully, he had not lost his sensitivity, good manners or impish sense of humour.

"What's the forecast, sir?" Sam laughed, "Sorry. Mr T."

"Set fair for a few days." Like all farmers, Frank kept a close eye on the weather. "The glass has been steady for over a week."

"Good." Sam looked at Annie before asking Frank, "Can we can take the boat out tomorrow? I've been dreaming of that for weeks."

"Of course, after milking, if you'd like to give a hand with that."

Sam grinned at him. "You know I will. How's Stella?"

Their conversation veered to the farm before tacking back to the Navy, finally ending when Frank got up from the table. "I must get back to work. Why don't you get changed while Annie clears away."

Sam's cheeky "Aye, aye sir" made Frank laugh as he went outside.

Sam decided Annie needed help with the clearing away, which somehow took much longer than it should have done because of frequent stops and exchanges of mutual affection.

Annie followed Sam upstairs when he went to get changed, thinking that he might need help. There was a moment in their long embrace when Sam was tempted to accept her kind offer but, thinking better of it, he gently shooed her out of his room.

The next ten days started each morning with milking the herd, followed by breakfast. After that Annie and Sam were free for the rest of the day. Time was all Frank could give them, a gift neither of them ever forgot.

Twice they packed a picnic and took the boat out. On the other days they walked with Aggie along the coast to a secluded cove tucked at the end of a narrow, wooded valley that a stream had cut through the cliff.

They were always back in time for the evening milking, after which they would make supper and talk with Frank about the farm and what they would do after the War. Occasionally they talked at the table, a large-scale map spread out and ideas and sketches scribbled into a notebook. Usually it was, as Frank said, "on the hoof," as they roamed the farm, always ending up at his favourite spot, leaning on the gate overlooking the sea.

They agreed where they would build a cottage for Sam's parents and Rachel, and another for Tante Mimi and Jannie, and that they might add a couple of rooms for holidaymakers to the farm, at least, that is what they told Frank. Annie really wanted them for the four children she and Sam planned to have.

Frank tried to convince Sam to spend a year at an agricultural college when the War ended, but neither he nor Annie thought much of that. He was always in bed by ten and never woke up when they crept upstairs much later.

Those ten days flew by. It is too painful to write about the day Sam left to join his ship; or their last day and night together. Grief, like love, is a private matter.

Chapter 49

HMS Persephone was a fast anti-aircraft cruiser of the Dido class, already a veteran of several actions in the Mediterranean.

Apprehension battled with excitement when Sam reported for duty. There was no time to dwell upon the homesickness that had gnawed at him the night before. He was shown to his messdeck, told where to stow his kit, "change into Number 3's, negative jumper" and "report to the forrard gangway."

Working parties were storing ship, chains of men passing boxes from hand to hand from lorries on the quay, up the gangway and into the ship. Others then took them below. It was heavy, repetitive work, enlivened by popular music played by the ship's Royal Marine band and the bawdy badinage of the seamen.

By 'pipe down' it was all Sam could do to stay awake in his hammock long enough to say a prayer for his extended family before kissing Martha's wedding ring, now back on a cord around his neck.

The next day was similar, though Sam was given a quick tour of the ship before being shown his action station – the port Oerlikon mounted on the aft end of the bridge superstructure.

Hands were turned to early on Wednesday morning, readying the ship for her move to a buoy in the stream where she would take on ammunition. Work ceased when the main broadcast clicked on. "D'ye hear there, this is the captain speaking. I regret to inform you of the loss of *HMS Eagle* yesterday afternoon......"

It was shattering news. Fear gripped Sam. The disbelief and anger in the faces of his messmates calmed him, as did the captain's assurance that "casualties were light."

There was a pause before the order "Carry on" was broadcast. Petty officers and leading seamen chivvied the hands back to work. There was no time to waste. Sam's induction into the Navy was full of such shocks as flesh is heir to.

Surprised by the broadcast, "Guns crews close up," Sam turned to a leading seaman. "Does that mean me?"

"Aye, lad. Quick as you can."

Sam raced up the ladder, checked his bearings and ran to his gun. "Are you da Souza?" a petty officer barked at him.

"Yessir."

"Strap yerself in." He handed him a headset – "It's plugged in" – before bawling at an out-of-breath lad, "Come on, Jones. Get that fuckin' magazine on."

Jones grinned at Sam. "Don't mind 'im, 'e's always like that."

Ignoring Jones, the PO ordered, "Make your report."

Sam clicked on his headset. "Port forrard Oerlikon closed up."

"Very good." A pause, "Load and stand by,"

"Load and stand by," Sam repeated before checking the safety catch was on and cocking the gun.

"Port Oerlikon loaded, sir."

The Gunnery Officer, remembering da Souza was new to the ship, explained, "There have been a number of hit and run raids. Engage enemy aircraft on sight." He paused again. "Understood?"

"Aye, aye, sir. Engage enemy aircraft on sight."

The petty officer tapped Sam on the shoulder. "You got that?"

When Sam nodded, he went on, "You won't 'ave time to think. Just remember your training – and fer fuck's sake make sure it's a Jerry."

The day passed in watches of acute tension alternating with sudden release when he changed places with his loader. It was hard not to be distracted by the constant flow of tugs and barges, until the gunnery officer reminded all guns' crews to stay alert. "If one aircraft gets through, we'll be spread across two counties. So concentrate."

They stayed on the buoy overnight, watch and watch about, taking on torpedoes in the morning before fuelling ship.

Persephone manoeuvred alongside under her own power on Thursday evening and leave was granted to one watch.

They sailed before dawn on Saturday 15th August in company with two destroyers. Because of the threat from submarines and aircraft, they remained in two watches and at defence stations for the passage south to Gibraltar. Sam rapidly adapted to life onboard and began to feel at home in the ship. He impressed the captain and gunnery officer with his accuracy with the Oerlikon during a practice shoot against a target towed by one of the destroyers; more importantly, he impressed the leading hand of his mess by the speed with which he fitted in.

Sam got drunk on his first run ashore in Gib, woke next morning with a screeching headache and vowed never to repeat the experience. A few days later his swift and instinctive shooting earned him the nickname, The Kid, after Billy the Kid, when he shot down his first aircraft. He got his second target when *Persephone* took part in Operation Torch, the Allied invasion of French North Africa in November.

Sam wrote to Jannie on both occasions. His first letter, full of satisfaction at avenging the deaths of Henri and Martha, saddened the old engineer. His second described how he imagined the terror of the aircrew when their aircraft caught fire and how he watched it struggling to gain height when it blew up.

His ending made Jannie and Miriam weep; "My heart is sick, Jannie, but I will keep doing my duty."

***

Persephone was torpedoed and sank with great loss of life on the night of 13th January 1943. As Miriam was still listed as Sam's next-of-kin, it was she who received the telegram regretting to inform her of the death of Ordinary Seaman Samuel da Souza. It was Miriam who had the terrible duty of informing Frank that his daughter's fiancé was dead; and it was the death of Sam that brought Lady Teagle to Saffron House soon after she heard the news from the Admiral's shore staff.

It was a sad afternoon, sharing memories, filling in gaps, mourning the tragically premature death of a singular young man. Emma was delighted by the news that Annie was carrying Sam's baby; "The very best gift he could give her." `She quizzed Miriam at great length about Annie and both of them about Martha's death and Frank, the farm and what sort of life the child might lead; all while the two women were subtly sizing each other up, to Jannie's quiet amusement.

Emma had not expected Miriam to be so well-educated, nor to have such a broad-minded approach to life. She steered the conversation towards life in the East End and the work the Cohens had been doing before Ike was killed, and was fascinated by the thought of the community centre in her synagogue. Mimi was pleased by Emma's interest, knowing from all Jannie and Sam had said that she was a warm, kind and generous person, unafraid to use her position and contacts to help people.

A friendship was born that afternoon which lasted until their deaths many years later.

As Emma was about to leave, Mimi remembered she still had the headscarf Emma had given Henri when he sailed for Dunkirk and which Jannie had taken from the pocket over Henri's heart when he was killed. She ran upstairs to fetch it.

"Here you are, my dear," handing the small package to Emma.

Emma paled. "I can't take that, Mimi," her voice husky as she pushed it away. "Give it to Annie." She nodded to herself. "For the baby." Smiling again, she said, "Tell her it comes with my love." Mimi strained to hear her next words, "It always did."

Chapter 50.

Annie gave birth to a beautiful baby girl in May 1943. Miriam and Jannie travelled to Cornwall for the second time in a few months because Annie insisted they were present at Martha Rachel's blessing. Having told them to wear stout shoes, Annie surprised them when she tucked her baby into a sling, handed a basket to her father and said, "It's not far." Frank laughed when he realised where she was taking them.

Annie had last come here a few days after telling her father she was pregnant. She smiled as she remembered how he'd wrapped his arms around her, kissed the top of her head and said, "Your mother would be delighted." She was not sure about that.

"Here we are," she whispered to her baby, "This is your daddy's and my very special place." Frank looked around the cove. It had not changed much since the days he had courted her mother there. He wondered if Annie realised that; she probably did.

"I'm not having a proper christening, Tante Mimi," Annie explained, "but I would like you and Jannie to bless Martha." She smiled shyly. "I'm not sure what you call it, but she's half Jewish. I don't think God will mind." Miriam blinked away her tears. "We call it a blessing, my dear, and I would be delighted."

"There's a little cup in the basket. Could you get some water from the stream?" She looked at Jannie for a moment before asking, "Will you name her, like they do in church?"

Jannie hesitated. "Are you sure? I'm not very holy."

Annie laughed. "Of course I'm sure." She put her hand on his. "Tante Mimi first, then you." Miriam took a pale blue silk headscarf from her bag and covered her hair before placing her hands on Martha's little head.

"May you be like Sarah, Rebecca, Rachel and Leah.

May God bless you and protect you.

May God show you favour and be gracious to you.

May God show you kindness and grant you peace."

She kissed Martha on her forehead, removed the scarf and gave it to Annie. "Give this to her when she is older. It comes from lady Teagle, with her love"

Jannie knelt on the sand, put the cup down and took the baby from Annie. Holding her in the crook of his left arm, he dipped two fingers into the water and drew the sign of the cross where Mimi had kissed her. "I name this baby Martha Rachel. May God bless her and all …" he coughed, thinking fast, "And all who know her."

Relieved, he gave Martha back to her mother. Gazing at her baby, Annie whispered, "Hello Martha Rachel da Souza."

So it came to pass that Martha Rachel was blessed in both faiths by the same God. Whether or not a priest or rabbi would agree did not concern them.

***

In December 1942 the whole world was stunned by the news that the Germans had killed over two million Jews.

The War in Europe dragged on to its inevitable, brutal conclusion.

About six million Jews were murdered by the Germans in what came to be known as the Holocaust. Among them were Sam, Ruth and Sarah's families. Jannie and Miriam were the first to know when they received Oom Paul's telegram telling them of the murder of Sam's family in a place called Auschwitz. Their nightly prayers for the safety of the da Souza family had not been answered.

Jannie replied to his old captain, "Will come as soon as possible."

It was not until July 1945 that he set foot on Dutch soil once more. Paul de Groot met Jannie at de Hoek. The old man had not weathered the storm of war well; the deaths of his friends had hit him hard. That, and the dreadful hunger of the past winter that had killed Joop, and almost killed him. It was only the fire of his implacable hatred of the man who had betrayed Simon, Judith and Rachel, that kept him alive.

"Come," he led Jannie to the station. "We can talk on the train." He had things to say he did not want his wife to hear when they got home.

Jannie was appalled to learn how a random choice of where to walk led to the unlikely coincidence of Andreas de Vink's son, Piet, passing the family on his bicycle. If Rachel had not recognised Sam's best friend and called out, if he had not told his father, if… if … if.

"No matter how many times I roll the dice, I cannot imagine ever coming up with the likelihood of this happening." Paul's tired eyes filled with tears. "Fate is so cruel."

Jannie stared out of the window, his mind blank.

Paul broke the long silence. "We will visit Betje tomorrow." He sighed. "It has been hard for her." He sighed again. "I should have insisted Dirk stay behind."

"No." Jannie's voice was sharp. "You must not think that." He put a hand on Paul's knee. "It was Dirk's decision, not yours." He paused. "Remember?"

Paul looked up. "You are right. But…"

"But nothing, Paul. We made our own choices." Jannie sounded angry.

"I know, Jannie. We did, for all the good it did us."

Jannie's laughter startled the old man.

"It did Henk and me a lot of good, Willem too." Jannie shook Paul gently, "Didn't it?"

Paul looked at Jannie for several seconds, his troubled face gradually relaxing into a smile. "It did, Jannie, it did indeed." He sat a little straighter. "You must tell us all about your wife, Henk's too."

"Ja, I will." Jannie looked around before lowering his voice. "I have a job for you, Kapitein."

"I can guess. Find de Vink."

"Ja. Find him. See if he has a routine, somewhere he always goes at the same time." Jannie lowered his voice. "He must not suspect he is being watched."

"I can arrange this." There was steel in Paul's voice. "It will be a pleasure."

He did not tell Jannie that he would ask Betje to do this. She had loved Sam since he first set foot onboard *De Ruyter*.

Admiral Sir William Teagle was delighted with his final appointment. As Commander-in-Chief Portsmouth, he flew his flag from *HMS Victory*, walked the same deck that Lord Nelson had walked and could dine where Nelson dined with his captains the night before Trafalgar.

Determined to acknowledge those with whom he had shared so many hard times, he asked Emma and his flag lieutenant to arrange a series of dinner parties onboard as a way of thanking them.

One such evening brought together the surviving crew of *De Ruyter*. At Emma's insistence Osborne, his steward, was also invited, and the invitation stipulated lounge suits. "Don't be stuffy, William, nobody has any money these days." She lit his cigar for him. "And if you can invite Petty Officer Willemsen, you can also invite the man who held you together every day of this bloody war."

The evening was a huge success, stories ebbed and flowed, tears mingled with laughter, toasts were drunk to Henri, Dirk and Sam, and to the future. After the table had been cleared and while the men went ashore for their cigars and port, Miriam and Emma walked on the upper deck, a little apart from the other ladies.

"We've found de Vink."

Emma gasped. "Really?"

"Yes, really. And he always travels from Rotterdam to Amsterdam on the same train on the same day every week."

"What are you going to do?"

"Shoot him." Speaking with more conviction than she felt, Miriam took a pace forward and stumbled on a deck fitting.

"Look at that," Emma stared at the deck, a hand to her mouth.

Miriam had tripped on the plate marking the spot where Nelson fell, mortally wounded by a French sharp-shooter.

Miriam shivered. "I hope he'd approve."

"Of course he would." Emma grasped Miriam's arm. "You can't do this on your own." Her eyes glinted. "I'm coming with you."

They shook hands over that sacred place and rejoined the others.

Miriam took Ike's service revolver deep into the woods a week later. She struggled to pull the hammer back before holding the butt with both hands and pulling the trigger. Appalled by the shattering noise and the violence of the recoil, she stuffed the gun in her pocket and hurried away, her ears ringing and wrists aching.

There was no such drama in Droxford. Emma's son Peter, knowing of her fascination with firearms, had given her the Beretta 9mm automatic pistol he had removed from the belt of a dead Italian officer. He also gave her the holster and a loaded spare magazine. Emma cleaned, test-fired and cleaned it again before locking the handgun in the gun cabinet.

William did not ask why Emma wished to accompany Miriam and Jannie when they went to Holland, but did insist that his long-serving steward, Osborne, went with her. "He's a wise old bird," he told her, "and may be able to keep you out of trouble."

Emma kissed the end of his nose. "Thank you, my love."

***

It was bitterly cold. No-one looked twice at the elderly woman as she ducked her head against the biting wind, a jaunty hat pinned firmly in place, her hands tucked into the thick fur of an old-fashioned muff, nor at her companion, equally well-wrapped against the weather.

The women hurried onto the platform before pausing to look around Rotterdam station. Emma leant towards Mimi. "That must be him. On the bench at the far end. Get a coffee."

Mimi hastened to the kiosk while Emma made her way slowly along the platform, pleased so few people were waiting for the train.

Jannie had paced out the distance to the bench two days ago and timed how long it took. Emma smiled at the memory of practising with him on the Embassy lawn. "Remember,' he said, "You're just an old lady waiting for her train."

Timing was critical. "You have to be sitting down just before the train pulls into the station. Get as close to de Vink as possible. Apologise in English. And don't forget to smile." Jannie had blushed as he added, "You have a beautiful smile."

He insisted on the double distraction of Miriam arriving a little later.

The plan worked perfectly. De Vink half rose as Emma sat down, lifting his hat briefly. Her "Thank you," in cut-crystal English enchanted him, as did the warmth of her smile.

"Ah, mevrouw," he replied, "I have not spoken English for many years."

Her reply was lost in a confusion of exhaust steam, squealing brakes and clanging buffers as the engine of the incoming train slowly passed, before coming to a halt a few yards further on.

Miriam put her mug on an empty bench and hurried towards them.

De Vink's eyes widened with pleasure when the attractive Englishwoman pressed her bosom against his arm as she turned to face him. He leant towards her, wondering at his good fortune, a smile creasing his fleshy face.

'You are Meneer de Vink?" she asked.

"Ja, mevrouw, how did you know?"

"You are famous, meneer. The notorious Jew hunter. Yes?"

"Ja." Suddenly uneasy, de Vink started to stand. Miriam arrived in time to hear him say, "It was my duty."

She pushed him back onto the seat, hissing, "You killed my family; da Souza. Remember them?"

Surrounded by steam, amid the noise of doors slamming, no-one noticed Emma jam her muff against de Vink's chest, nor heard the two sharp retorts of the Beretta concealed therein.

He grunted as he slumped onto the bench. Motionless, the women watched de Vink struggle to say something before exhaling noisily. Miriam put her ungloved hand on his neck. "He is dead."

Emma stood and straightened her coat. Moving away, they strolled slowly through the steam to an open gate and onto the road. Neither said a word.

Miriam turned left to find a tram stop. Emma removed her distinctive hat and muff, pocketing them before tying a plain brown headscarf beneath her chin. She turned right and walked around the corner to the waiting taxi. A cloud of cigar smoke wafted out when Jannie opened his door. There was no chance of the driver noticing the slight smell of gunpowder and scorched fur.

***

The quiet group of elderly people attracted little attention as they boarded the *Prague* next morning. Their few bags were carried onboard by a steward and placed in the purser's office at the request of the Embassy.

Jannie and Osborne went into the first-class lounge with the two women where they were greeted by the Chief Steward, escorted to a table and helped into their chairs. Coffee was served. "Bit of a treat, milady," Osborne remarked, passing a plate of biscuits to her.

"Make the most of it, Percy." Jannie interjected. "She'll work your socks off when we get back."

They went on deck just before 0900 to watch the ship slip and proceed to sea. It was just another departure for the crew, but a moment of profound significance for them.

Mimi, her arm tucked under Jannie's, leant against him as they walked slowly aft and murmured, "Do you think we'll ever come back?"

"Not unless you want to. There's nothing here for me." Jannie had said his farewells to Holland five years ago. "It would be different if Sam or Henri were alive, or Simon and Judith. Too many ghosts walk these streets today."

He stopped, put his arms around her and held her for a long time before saying, "We have each other, my dearest. That is enough."

They kissed tenderly, and then with a sudden, urgent passion.

"Don't get any ideas, Percy." Emma nudged the Chief Steward and walked on. Osborne sniffed loudly.

Mimi and Jannie joined them at the taffrail where they stood in silence, watching Holland disappear into the mist.

The ship was picking up speed as she cleared the sandbanks and headed into deeper water. Emma looked across at Jannie. "Why don't you and Percy get another coffee. We'll join you in a minute or two."

Emma and Miriam turned as if to watch them leave, while actually checking to make sure there was no-one else on deck.

"It's a good job it's cold," Emma observed, turning back to gaze at the wake boiling below them. She took the Beretta from her pocket. "I shan't be wanting this again." Emma stared at the gun in its polished leather holster before dropping it overboard.

"Nor I this."

Emma was astonished to see Miriam haul an enormous revolver from her handbag.

She spat on it before tossing the gun into the sea with an anguished "Damn you, de Vink."

"That was our wretched duty," she sobbed, "But it won't bring them back."

Emma and Miriam embraced, their tears flowing as the ship turned, heeling slightly before steadying on her course for Harwich.

Osborne noticed their reddened eyes and went to the bar.

He gave them each a glass of brandy. "The wind is cold now. It will soon change."

The End

Postscript

"So that's where it went," Peter mused, quietly astonished by what he had read in his mother's diaries. "I did wonder why it wasn't in its place in the gun cabinet."

He looked again at an old newspaper cutting he had found tucked in one of them. The murder of a Jew-hunter had only warranted a few lines.

That afternoon he went up to his mother's bedroom. He was examining her muff when Osborne came in.

"She was a remarkable woman, your mother. They both were."

Acknowledgements and thanks

With my grateful thanks to:

My editor, Jo Smith, for her meticulous attention to detail and for the kind and gentle way in which she guided my story from submission to publication;

Jennifer Tuson for her careful proof-reading;

Bettany Wilson for the cover design;

Ian Hooper, my publisher, for turning my dream into reality;

Jo Fitzgerald and Emma Ellis for their support and encouragement and

my wife of fifty years, Philippa, for listening patiently to every word of the story, several times.

Author's notes

This is a work of fiction anchored by historical events, and by locations, most of which I have visited, stayed at or lived in.

It is dedicated to Jennefer Tobin who twice raised me out of the depths of despair. She allowed me to feature her home of many years, 17 Wilkes Street, in this and the previous story, *A Flower in Winter*. Here, as everywhere she lived, she worked tirelessly to improve the safety and conditions of service of British Merchant Navy personnel. Her brainchild, *Tobin Tagging*®, is designed to improve standards of safety in merchant ships around the world.

Although Saffron House is fictional, there is a place in Hampshire to which it has some similarity.

Nanjigga Farm is loosely based on a farm in West Cornwall where my wife's ancestors lived and worked for some 125 years, between approximately 1750 and about 1875. By happy coincidence, it is also where Jo Fitzgerald used to live and where she told me about her relative, Sim Gokkes and his family. Their murder in Auschwitz in 1943 inspired me to write *A Flower in Winter* and this book.

I have heard a story about a German aircraft shooting up a threshing machine at the farm but am unable to find any records of that attack.

About the Author

While a student at Portsmouth Technical College, David was tempted to follow his heart and become a writer. Instead, having been brought up in a service family, duty called and he joined the Royal Navy as a seaman officer.

In 1971 he left the Senior Service to pursue his other dream - of becoming a professional civilian sailor.

Hard years followed before he was sufficiently experienced and qualified to captain groups of young Londoners on adventurous sailing voyages in a traditional old Norwegian sailing rescue ship.

In 1977 David was recruited to run Ocean Youth Club, Britain's largest sail training fleet. In 1985 he was head-hunted by the Drake Fellowship which he soon merged with Fairbridge to create Fairbridge-Drake. This became the UK's most effective motivational training charity for unemployed young people in inner cities.

David eventually left London for West Cornwall, where, at the age when most people retire, his wife suggested opening a bookshop. They transformed a local tea-room into a much-loved café and second-hand bookshop where David started writing poetry again, publishing *Any Cornish Beach* in 2009.

David relished the solitude imposed by the Covid lockdown and began to write his first novel, *A Flower in Winter*. It was published in 2024 and is the prequel to *Out of the Depths*.

www.ingramcontent.com/pod-product-compliance
Lightning Source LLC
Chambersburg PA
CBHW032011180726
48283CB00008B/2633